THE BOOK OF REVENGE

A MATT MARDELL CRIME STORY

LINDA DUNSCOMBE

LUNCH TIME LIBRARY

THE BOOK OF REVENGE is Copyrighted material

Written by: Linda Dunscombe

Published by: Lunch Time Library

Cover designed by Get Covers

eBook preparation: Peter Dunscombe

Copyright © 2013 by Linda Dunscombe

All rights reserved.

No part of this book may be reproduced in any form or by any electronic or mechanical means, including information storage and retrieval systems, without written permission from the author, except for the use of brief quotations in a book review.

This book is a work of fiction. Names, characters and incidents are the product of the author's imagination or are used fictitiously. Any resemblance to actual persons, living or dead, is entirely coincidence.

❦ Created with Vellum

FOREWORD

The Book of Revenge
A DI Matt Mardell Crime Story

'I HAD NEVER KILLED ANYONE BEFORE'

Matt fights crime, but his real enemy is himself.

His marriage is in tatters, his best friend is a bottle of whisky and a killer is in his town.

Murders are making the headlines. Is it drugs, or a serial killer? Or is it something worse? Much worse. Matt knows the victims; he knows what links them all together.

Matt is forced to face the past head on. Does it always have to be accounted for? He is beginning to believe that it does, if he doesn't find the killer soon, the killer will be finding him.

1

CHAPTER ONE

'I had never killed anyone before'

He was on his knees on the dirty floor. The place was a shit hole. I could smell his fear, and I hadn't expected that. I'd read somewhere that during extreme stress all your senses go into hyper-drive. It was true. I was acutely aware of every sound and every movement. I had a strange sensation of time slowing down, like every second lived lasted a minute. The man smelt of sweat and urine and something else, something that I knew instinctively was the stench of fear, some primitive chemical signal sent out by his body.

I threw the lipstick onto the floor. He glanced up at me, just briefly. I nodded my head towards it. So he picked the lipstick up and removed the small piece of paper wrapped around it with an elastic band. His hands were shaking violently as he unfurled the note and read the message. He looked up at me again, but without making eye contact. His gaze focused on my chin and I felt a surge of anger. Was he such a coward that he couldn't even look into the eyes of his executioner?

'You want me to write?' he said, his voice little more than a rasping sound.

I pointed to the floor. He took the lipstick lid off and fiddled for a few seconds until he twisted the tip out enough to do the job.

He started to form the letters; it wasn't easy on the cheap grimy lino. He was working against months, maybe years of ground in grease and dirt. The lipstick smudged, and he was struggling to keep his hand steady.

Noises from the street outside were making me nervous. Drunken shouts, cars, I even heard the sounds of a siren. But I had to keep calm, keep control. It was a rough neighbourhood. The part of my brain, still capable of being rational, knew that the noises were normal. I took a few deep breaths, forced myself to be strong. My hand holding the gun was steady.

I could do this.

He finished writing and looked up at me again. Hope was in his eyes. He'd completed the task. Surely his reward would be mercy.

But I had no mercy in my soul.

I took aim, and I fired.

In the fraction of a second it took for the bullet to make contact with his head, I saw his hope turn to disbelief and then to terror and finally...

Well, I'm not sure what the final fleeting emotion or thought was. I hope it was recognition, understanding, or acceptance.

I froze for a few seconds. Hit by the enormity of what I had just done. But once again, my rational brain saved me.

Chapter 1

On autopilot, I picked up the elastic band and the note. Careful not to step in any blood, I quickly left the flat.

I don't think anybody saw me leave. I heard a door open in the flat above me and footsteps on the stairs. But I didn't look back. Outside on the street, I removed the balaclava and walked quickly past the row of rundown terrace houses and round the next bend. I'd gone little more than a hundred yards before the shaking started, and just a few steps later I was on my knees throwing up into the gutter.

It made me feel a little better.

The streets were empty. It was late, or early, technically a new day. I blended in. I looked like just another drunk, staggering home. Nobody took any notice of me.

One more corner and I would be safe.

Was I pleased? Probably not. In all my mental practice runs, I felt a tremendous surge of emotions, including satisfaction and elation. But the reality was a lot flatter. I did what had to be done. I wanted him to suffer, to be sorry, maybe even to plead or beg for his life. But in reality he had been a pathetic rat, trapped in a rat hole. I almost felt I had done both him and society a service by ending his wretched, worthless existence, and that wasn't what I wanted. I needed to feel that I had robbed the man of a life worth living. That depriving him of a future was a fair judgment and a fitting punishment.

I knew I was being hard on myself. All the anticipation, all the preparation, maybe an anti-climax was inevitable. He was only the first. Hopefully, the next from the list would satisfy my need for revenge.

2

CHAPTER TWO

Matt Mardell reached for the bedside lamp. He found the switch and groaned as his eyes squinted in protest at the brightness of the light and the noise of the stupid ringtone on his mobile phone.

'Jen, it's ...' he glanced at the alarm clock, 'the middle of the sodding night. If someone isn't dead, then you soon will be.'

Hearing her response, he ended the call, and with resignation he climbed out of bed. An empty bottle of whisky was on the floor and he winced as he stubbed his toe on it. He picked the phone up again and pressed speed-dial. 'Jen? Better send a car...'

Matt climbed into yesterday's clothes. Picking them up from the bedroom floor, he had no memory of dropping them there. He glimpsed himself in the wardrobe mirror and wished he hadn't. He ran his fingers through his hair; it didn't help. 'Bugger,' he groaned.

He left the bathroom looking much the same as he had when he'd entered. But at least his mouth didn't feel like he'd swallowed sawdust anymore. He pushed open the door to the spare room. It was empty. Doubting the evidence of his own eyes, he switched the light on. The bed looked like nobody had used it. He wondered if he should worry about her safety. Her behaviour had been erratic lately. But she was an adult, and although he was still her husband, he certainly wasn't her keeper. He switched the light off and closed the door.

Downstairs, Matt put the kettle on and checked through the window that the car wasn't already waiting. He knew he had little chance of making and drinking a coffee before his lift arrived. But he needed caffeine, and it was worth a try.

He spooned in the sugar and stirred. What he really wanted to do was add a dash of brandy to kick start his brain, but he resisted. He managed a sip before he heard a car pull up outside. He took a long slurp and burnt his mouth. The day, or more accurately, the night, was not going well.

The front door opened. His tired and fuzzy brain registered that it was wrong; the driver wouldn't have a key. Matt hurried into the hall as his wife staggered through the doorway, smiled inanely at him, and promptly threw up over his shoes.

MATT CLIMBED out of the car. Jen Tyson had everything under control. She was young, ambitious, beautiful and bright. In Matt's opinion, she represented all that was unjust in the world. How was it fair that one person got everything? And why did it have to be her? It wasn't even that he didn't like her. Since arriving in town three months ago, she had settled into the job; she was friendly and keen, pleasant and never rude. The problem was his; he knew that. All her bright shiny perfection made him feel jaded, bitter, and, if brutally honest with himself, a failure.

The flat was in a rundown converted Victorian terrace, on the wrong side of town. Not that there was really a right side of town. Bidbury was one of those places that prosperity forgot to touch. Anyone sensible who made a success of life got out the minute they could, and if they stayed they moved to the villages on the outskirts of the town. But even by Bidbury standards, this was the bottom of the neighbourhood pile.

They cordoned the area off. Police cars, blue lights, suited and booted Socos going about their business. Jen waved him in. Despite the early hour, she was immaculate and perky. Matt groaned. He seemed to do a lot of that lately. He looked around the room with the eyes of a man who'd seen it all before. Humanity in all its foulest glory. He wrinkled his nose, an involuntary response to the smell of violent death, and looked down at the body on the dirty floor bathed in a pool of blood.

'Sorry...'

Matt looked at Jen. She pointed to the smudged writing on the floor. 'Think that's what it says.'

'Well, I guess he is now. Do we know who he is?'

A uniformed officer spoke from behind them. 'Odell, sir.'

Matt swung round to face the officer. 'Adam Odell?'

The officer checked his notebook and nodded.

'You know him, Gov?' Jen asked.

Matt kept quiet, not ready to answer. Adam Odell. He ran the name through his mind. Looking at the corpse on the floor and the grotty hole he apparently lived in, he couldn't believe the man had once been a promising athlete.

Chapter 2

Never one to keep quiet, Jen asked again. 'Know him Gov?'

Slowly, Matt nodded his head. 'User and dealer...'

'Knew it.'

Matt raised a skeptical eyebrow.

'Well, dump like this. Nothing worth nicking, it had to be drugs really, didn't it?' She said. 'I mean, why else would anyone kill a loser like him?'

Matt didn't answer. He knew a small voice kept under lock and key in some dark corner of his brain, might have some view on the matter. But the door restraining that voice was staying firmly shut.

'Yeah, almost certainly drugs,' he said flatly before turning to the uniformed officer. 'Any sign of a break-in?'

'No, sir. Whoever did this apparently walked in through the door.'

'A punter then,' Jen said, pleased. 'A deal gone bad.'

'Witnesses? Surely someone heard the shot? Who found him?'

'Guy upstairs,' Jen replied. 'He heard a noise, came down to investigate. The door was open, and he found the body, but he didn't see anyone leave.'

Matt took one last look around the sad, grubby room. Then he looked at Jen. 'First light. Check all the neighbours. Get the lippy to forensics, pull all the data on Odell, and find out his known associates...'

Jen looked satisfied. 'Treat it as drug related then?'

'For now,' Matt answered, not totally convinced. He headed for the door.

'Are you going to the station, Gov?'

'Nope,' Matt replied. 'I'm going home, I need my beauty sleep.'

'Can't argue with that Gov,' Jen said, quietly. The uniformed officer stifled a snigger.

Matt held his tongue and left the flat. As he walked towards the squad car, a rumble of thunder preceded the first drops of heavy rain. He was tired, and a bit hung over. But it wasn't really sleep he needed. He knew he had been avoiding reality for far too long. It was time he confronted his wife. Time they sat down and talked. He had a strong feeling that he wouldn't like what he heard.

3

CHAPTER THREE

There was a removal van parked on the drive and a sold sign in the front garden. It was a pleasant house, not rich or ostentatious, but a comfortable three bedroom detached. Liz Bryant was directing the removal men as they manoeuvred her cream sofa through the narrow front door. The man in the garden next door, who was mowing the lawn, watched her while his wife pretended to weed her immaculate flowerbeds.

With the sofa safely into the lounge, Liz plonked herself down and looked around her new home. Her teenage daughter, Sam, came in wearing an enormous smile, followed by a tall lad, her boyfriend, Craig. 'Mum, this is great.'

Liz smiled, 'your room ok?'

'I love it.'

Craig put his arm around Sam's shoulders. 'Sorry babe, but we've gotta go.' He looked at Liz, 'it's the final; I'll be in trouble if I don't show.'

'Who am I to stand in the way of football,' Liz said. 'Go on, get going.'

CHAPTER THREE

She stood up and followed the pair outside. The removal men were struggling with a large antique looking desk. 'Put it in the room straight in front of you at the top of the stairs,' She said. One of them groaned. It was a heavy desk. Liz watched as they edged it through the doorway. She didn't want it damaged.

Keeping a wary eye on the progress of the desk, she watched as Craig headed towards a motorbike parked beside the van; he lifted two helmets, put one on his head and strapped it under his chin. She didn't much like her daughter riding pillion, but she knew that like mothers everywhere, all she could do was keep her fingers crossed. Locking her daughter up to keep her safe was never really a viable option. And as young lads went, Craig seemed to be one of the better ones.

Sam hung back. 'I can stay if you want mum. Get the coach back to Uni on Monday.'

'Don't be silly, I'll be fine.' Liz made sure her voice was steady and confident. She smiled warmly at her daughter. 'Go...'

Sam hugged her tightly and pulled back to look directly into her eyes. 'New start, mum?'

Liz nodded her head. Tears were threatening to fall, but she kept her composure. Her daughter let her go and hurried to the motorbike. Liz followed more slowly. She took a deep steadying breath before she spoke. 'Thanks for your help.'

Craig answered while Sam tightened her helmet. 'No worries, Lizzie. Make sure next time I come you have the gear set up,' he grinned, '... you are in for a thrashing lady.'

Liz laughed. 'In your dreams...' she retaliated, while mentally searching the packed boxes for the Playstation and games.

Chapter 3

The bike roared away with Sam frantically waving. Liz watched them go, wondering, as she had a hundred times before, where the years had gone. But she didn't have time for nostalgia or melancholy; she had a house to organise. So she directed the rest of her furniture off the van and watched as it drove away. With the show over, the neighbours finished their fake gardening and went inside. Finally alone, Liz went back outside and unlocked her car. Liz opened the boot and took out a large box. She lifted it up; it was heavy. `She relocked the car and carried it into the house, balancing it on her hip. She only got to the second step on her way upstairs when the front doorbell rang. With some irritation, she put the box on the floor. Not happy with leaving it there, she opened a door to an under-stairs cupboard and pushed it inside. The doorbell rang again. Someone was getting impatient. Liz hurried across and opened the front door.

Her best friend, Dawn, was on the doorstep holding a bunch of flowers so huge they virtually hid her face. Liz's irritation dissolved as she took the flowers and got immediately squashed by an enormous hug. Dawn was a dancer and everything about her screamed the fact. She was dainty and floated around on ridiculously high heels.

A tall, dark, equally elegant man, Phillip, followed Dawn into the hall and looked around him. 'This is really cool, Lizzie.'

Liz smiled her thanks; she was fond of Phillip and knew how her best friend felt about him. She had an entire house worth of boxes to unpack, but was glad of the temporary distraction. Besides, the only person she loved more in the world than Dawn was Sam.

'It's lovely, Lizzie.' Dawn said before turning to Phillip and playfully tapping his arm, 'nobody says cool anymore.'

CHAPTER THREE

'They don't?'

'Nope.'

Liz smiled as she led them into the kitchen.

'So what's the new cool then?' Phillip asked.

'Sick, I think.'

Liz put the kettle on.

'I'm impressed.' Dawn said, as she looked at the mugs and coffee already unpacked. There was even a loaf of bread and the toaster on the side. 'You're really organised, Lizzie.'

Liz shrugged. 'You know what tradesfolk are like; they need regular caffeine to keep them at it.' She poured boiling water into the mugs and stirred in instant coffee and milk. 'Haven't found the percolator yet...'

Dawn laughed and took the offered mug. 'It takes time to settle. No regrets?'

'No.' Liz wondered briefly if it was true, but quickly dismissed the thought.

'So when are you going to tell me why?'

'Why what?' Liz asked, pretending not to understand.

'Oh come on Lizzie, this is me. I know you grew up here, but it's not home is it. I mean all your friends, top of the list being me, are an hour's drive away now.'

Liz shrugged. What could she say? How could she explain?

'It was all too familiar...' she said, trying to simplify and articulate the complex feelings of loss and sadness that had shadowed her for so long.

She looked out of the window to the garden. Phillip had wandered out of the back door and was chatting across the fence to the neighbour's teenage daughter. 'What's happening with you and Phillip?'

Dawn allowed the subject to be changed and followed

Chapter 3

Liz's gaze. 'Oh, just more of the same sad story. Older woman falls for younger man and all that crap.'

Liz smiled, but she knew her friend's pain was very real. 'Only a few years older…'

'Ten.'

'So cut him loose.' Liz said.

Dawn shook her head sadly. 'One day you'll realise that one thing in life we have no control over is love.'

'Rubbish, of course we do.'

'Nope. If I could write a list describing the man, I want to love. Santa would not be putting Phil in my stocking!'

They both looked out of the window. Phillip was teaching the pretty young girl to Cha-cha.

Dawn looked at Liz, 'one day you'll understand.'

Liz sipped her coffee she knew it would never happen to her.

4

CHAPTER FOUR

Matt stood up from his desk. Jen was still head down, hard at work. He felt a pang of guilt and regret. Had he ever been as diligent and dedicated as she was? He grabbed his jacket from the back of the chair and said a general, 'see you tomorrow,' to the room. Maybe he was being too hard on himself. He was only thirty-seven; he'd made Detective Inspector four years ago. That was pretty good going. Trouble was, now he didn't really know what he was doing or why he was doing it. In the early days he'd always had a clear vision. He'd been idealistic and had wanted to make a difference, to clear the streets of the bad guys. It had all seemed so black and white then. But with each passing year, the shades of grey were now blurring this vision.

Matt headed for his car. He should go straight home. His determination to talk to his wife that morning had failed. Avril had been sound asleep in the spare room and his attempt to rouse her for work had resulted in her throwing the alarm clock at his head. Luckily, she'd missed, but the bruise on his shoulder showed her aim wasn't that far off.

Chapter 4

He looked across the road at the pub. The police station was at the top of the high street and The George was a favourite after work drinking hole. He used to kid himself that by nipping in for a pint or two after work it kept him in with the locals. And he had heard snippets and chanced upon information across the years that had been useful. But the pint or two had turned to three or four or five. He wasn't an alcoholic; at least he didn't think he was he could stop, if he wanted to. But life was pretty crap at the moment, and he needed something to help him through.

Matt decided that since he wasn't ready to go home and he wanted to avoid another drinking session, maybe a workout was what he needed. He pulled out a sports bag that, like him, had seen better days from the boot and locked the car. He walked across the road, passed the pub and headed down the high street.

It was closing time, nothing as modern as late night opening in Bidbury. Some shops even had a midweek half-day closing. He sometimes felt as though it had caught him in a time warp. If only he could escape the town, and the past that trapped him in it, another reality could be his. The door of the shoe shop opened and the manager, Andrew Martin, stepped out. A pretty young girl who followed him out, hurried off, watched by Andrew.

Matt and Andrew briefly acknowledged each other. It was Matt who looked away first, as it always was. He knew as he walked away that the man would be smirking; the thought filled him with fury. He mocked himself with the irony. He'd joined the force because of Andrew and men like him, yet it was his job that prevented him from wiping the sick, smug smile from the man's lips. Matt hurried on.

The Gym was all shiny and new. Shimmering glass and chrome, which was totally at odds with the rest of the town.

CHAPTER FOUR

Outside were posters of impossibly beautiful men and women, advertising the figure you really, really want.

Matt glanced at them as he walked past, 'yeah, you too, can be air-brushed to perfection,' he muttered to himself.

It was a busy time for the gym. Full of people leaving work and dropping in for a swim or a class or workout before heading home. Matt knew most of them. That's what happened when you lived your entire life in one place. He was on the treadmill running for his life, his breathing was laboured and sweat was dripping onto his shirt. Matt had to face it; he was not the fit young man he used to be.

A woman walked into the gym. She paused, taking in the scene and its occupants. Matt saw her in the oversize mirror that stretched the length of the room. She walked towards the treadmills and stepped onto the one next to Matt. He watched as she started at a slow, warm up jog and realised he hadn't seen her before; he glanced her way and smiled a greeting, although he wondered if it appeared as more like a grimace since he was so out of breath.

The woman was slowly increasing her speed. She looked calm and fit. Her breathing was even and in control, and the speed kept climbing.

Matt, well aware of the woman running beside him, was trying, and failing, to keep pace. While he huffed and puffed in increasing agony, she might as well be on a walk in the park. Forced to concede defeat, he slowed down and climbed off the treadmill. He looked across at her as she continued to run at a fast, steady pace with a satisfied smile on her face.

Showered and dressed, Matt stood outside the gym, leaning against the glass puffing on a cigarette. She came out through the electric doors. She looked good. Made up and dressed up, ready for a night out.

Matt, surprised by these feelings of envy he felt towards whoever her date was, looked up.

She paused, looked at the cigarette in his hand, raised a perfectly shaped eyebrow, smiled and then walked on.

Matt stubbed the cigarette out and hurried after her. 'Down to three a day now.'

'What's the point?' she asked, without slowing or stopping.

The question surprised Matt. He thought about it. 'No point at all, I suppose. It's been a tough day and I like it.'

She gave him a 'whatever' shrug and kept on walking.

'Haven't seen you in there before, are you new?'

'Yep.'

'You've done that before, though.'

'Yep.'

Matt was getting mildly irritated with himself as well as with her. What was he doing? He didn't go around trying to pick up women. It wasn't even like she was interested. But still he walked along beside her. They reached the edge of the town's main car park and she stopped beside a blue Mini. She pressed a remote control to unlock the door and Matt opened the driver's door and held it while she climbed in. For some strange reason, he didn't want to let her go. 'I'll see you again?'

'You might,' she said, as she started the engine.

Matt shoved his hand forward. 'Matt Mardell.'

She paused for a second, and then she took his hand and shook it. 'Liz Bryant.' She closed the door and drove away, leaving him grinning like an idiot.

Matt whistled as he walked up the drive to his house. He opened the front door and entered just as Avril was about to leave.

CHAPTER FOUR

'You're late,' she said, with more indifference than annoyance.

'I stopped at the gym.'

'Dinner's in the bin,' she said. 'Don't wait up.'

Matt reached out a hand towards her. 'We've got to talk...' But she had gone. The door slammed on his words.

CHAPTER FIVE

The man was in his pyjamas. Expensive silk material that was stretched large enough to cover his enormous fat belly. I was standing on the landing but could see him through the open door. He was sitting on the king-size bed watching a late night chat show. He had a large glass of whisky in one hand and a tv remote in the other. It couldn't be more different from the last one. This was an expensive house in a village just outside of town. This guy was a solicitor, and he had a fat cat life style. He'd done well for himself. Clearly he hadn't let the past hold him back. I took a step closer, and a floorboard gave a little moan.

He paused the TV, and called out, 'Tina?'

I stood still and held my breath. Obviously he got no response. The TV volume went back on and I breathed again. I knew Tina was his wife, and that this was her bridge night. I also knew that she only played bridge until eight thirty, and then she went to her lover's house and spent the next three hours with him. She wouldn't be home before midnight, which suited me just fine as I had no quarrel with her.

The man climbed off the bed and walked into the en-suite. When he walked back into the room a few minutes later, I was waiting. He froze when he saw me, his eyes fixed on the gun. I waved it at him and he followed my instruction and fell to his knees.

'No! Please. I have money, you want money? I'll open the safe. Yes, the safe. You can have it all…'

I wasn't interested in the safe, or his money. But it gave me some small satisfaction that he considered his life worth pleading or paying for.

He didn't want to comply. But a gun is a powerful incentive. He asked me why? A tiny word, but I couldn't answer other than with the shot that ended his life.

I wanted to tell him. I wanted to tell everyone. But I couldn't, not yet. Not until it was over. Then everyone would know why.

I felt a massive surge of anger at his question, and I suppose a feeling of vindication. Not that I needed it. I knew what I was doing was right. The man should have known it. In his heart he should have known that this day would come. The past always has to be paid for.

6

CHAPTER SIX

Matt had an unlit cigarette in one hand and an unopened bottle of whisky in the other. He looked as bad as he felt - a tormented man. His mobile phone rang. He looked at the clock. Twenty past midnight. With a sigh and a deep breath, he put the bottle down and answered it. 'Jen, don't you ever sleep?'

'Gotta another one boss,' she replied.

MATT LOOKED DOWN at the body. An icy chill seeped into his bones. He knew what it was. That voice he kept locked away in his head was screaming and hammering on the door to be let loose. He ignored the voice and fought the fear.

'Same killer Gov.' Jen said, pointing to the writing, which was on the wall this time, low down as though the victim had scrawled it while on his knees. 'Do you think we've got a serial killer...?'

Matt looked at his younger colleague. She could barely hide her excitement at the prospect. 'We don't know what we've got yet; it's too early to tell.' He replied, pleased that his voice didn't reveal his own inner turmoil.

'Did the victims know each other?' She said. 'Dope-head and a solicitor, user and supplier maybe?'

Matt looked around the room, his eyes stopped at the writing. Big sprawling letters 'SORRY' written in capitals, and not very well. The writer's hand was probably shaking. Not surprising with a gun to his head. The killer was a very good shot, one bullet fired into the forehead, execution style.

'No break in again,' Jen said. 'The victims must know the killer. What links it all together?' She walked across to stand beside Matt. 'And what do they all have to be sorry about?'

That was a question that Matt hardly dared to ask. Adam Odell was dead. Now Edward Sharp was a bloody mess on his bedroom floor. Were they random victims of a killer with a grudge against humanity? Or were they handpicked individuals paying for crimes in their past?

'The lipstick must be significant,' Jen said. 'We should get a forensics report from the Odell killing soon. It looks to me like cheap, over the counter, available everywhere makeup.'

Matt felt tired, pissed off, and more than a little rattled. He had a horrible hunch creeping up on him. He just hoped to god that he was wrong.

7

CHAPTER SEVEN

Kylie Martin stayed under the duvet even though her alarm clock was ringing loudly. She didn't want to get up, didn't want to face a new day. Her Dad was up, she could hear him downstairs. He'd been out till the early hours. Again. Not that she cared. It meant he was tired and probably drunk. Anything that kept him away from her was fine.

She pushed the covers off and grudgingly climbed out of bed. She glanced at her clock; it was nearly eight. He would leave at about twenty past. Trouble was if she left it until then to go downstairs she wouldn't have time for breakfast, or time to make her lunch, before she had to leave. Not that she cared about being late for school. But her form tutor, Ms Low, was a bitch and would tell her dad. Any excuse to get him into the school. Kylie was pretty sure the bitch had a thing for him. Rumour was the Lilo, as her students called her, had a bit of a thing for anything under fifty with a dick. Her tummy rumbled, but she'd just have to grab a banana on her way out.

Kylie moved a chair away from the door. Although it was

a heavy computer chair, it wasn't much of a barrier. But just having it pushed against there, gave her the illusion of safety. Kylie opened the door slowly and peeped onto the landing. A squat, thickset, unspeakably ugly dog was outside her door, growling menacingly. Her dad had forgotten to shut Bruce in the garden. The brute would stay outside her room all day now, keeping her prisoner until her father came home again. Kylie closed her door, pushed the chair back into position. Her stomach moaned, complaining it was empty, and she needed to pee. But what could she do? She crawled back into bed and pulled the duvet over her head, closing her eyes.

8

CHAPTER EIGHT

Andrew watched as a couple of young girls were trying on strappy shoes. They should have been at school, but were clearly bunking off. He straightened his hair and popped a mint chewing gum into his mouth. A well-built man who knew he still looked good as he approached the big four zero. What he didn't know was that up close, he looked worn with hard eyes and thin lips. He fancied himself as a charmer. He was wrong.

He crossed the shop floor to approach the girls. His assistant, seventeen-year-old Gemma, was helping them. 'Gemma, the stock room needs dusting. I'll deal with these pretty wenches,' he grinned, pleased with his ability to be witty and charming.

Gemma pulled a face at the girls that made it very clear what she really thought of him. The girls laughed in agreement.

Suitably encouraged, he thought they were responding to him rather than laughing at him. 'Be a sweetie, Gemma, and make me a coffee,' he said to her departing back. He looked at the girls and smiled his best smile, which was just plain creepy, 'lots of perks to being the big boss.'

The two girls exchanged a look. Silent communication completed, they got up and left. Andrew's eyes lingered on their very short skirts. 'Sluts,' he muttered, as he watched them go.

9

CHAPTER NINE

Matt saw Liz as she entered the car park. Her head was down; she was walking towards her car. He knew the sensible thing to do was to walk away, and fast. His infatuation, or whatever made him chase after her, was a complication he could really do without.

He watched her climb into her car; he sped up. It was like she had attached him to an invisible elastic cord and every time he saw her she drew him in.

She was sitting in the driver's seat, but the engine wasn't running. She seemed to be fixated on the car park ticket machine. A traffic warden approached the machine, and she seemed to wake up suddenly from her daydream. She glanced at the dashboard clock, Matt guessed her ticket must be about to expire. He looked towards the warden and saw that another man had approached. It was Andrew Martin; they seemed to be involved in a heated argument. There was a lot of shouting and hand waving. Matt watched as Andrew pushed the warden who stumbled backwards but kept on his feet, hurling back abuse Andrew Martin stormed off.

Show over, Matt knocked on her window and watched as she jumped in surprise. He bent down, grinning at her through the glass. Disappointed that the first expression he saw on her face was irritation, quickly hidden with a smile.

'There's a law against stalking,' she said, as the electric window slid down.

He tried to look serious, but was sure he failed. 'Call a police officer. Tell you what; I'll do it for you.' Matt whipped his warrant card from his pocket and flashed it at her.

'An Inspector, I'm impressed. Am I under arrest, officer?'

'Depends,' he said, enjoying himself. 'Have you done anything wrong?'

Liz looked like she was thinking hard. 'Nope, not today...'

'Well, loitering in a public place could look suspicious, anti-terrorism laws and all that.'

Liz looked suitably concerned, her face was serious, but she couldn't hide the amusement in her eyes, 'sorry officer.'

Matt grinned. 'Have a drink with me tonight and I'll let you off this time.'

10

CHAPTER TEN

James Tate climbed off his pedal bike and pushed it through his back gate. He leant it against the wall, closed the gate and locked it, then headed into the house through the back door. He felt tired; it had been a long day. Looking older than his thirty-seven years; time had not been kind to him. He hung his coat on the hook in the hall and carried on into the lounge. It was a small, poorly furnished room, in need of decoration and not even that clean. His job as a traffic warden didn't win him any popularity prizes. Nor did it give him a life of luxury. But it kept a roof over him and his daughter's head, and in a life that had little else to commend it, Annie was his world.

The TV was on. His mother-in-law, Paula - or more accurately, his ex-mother-in-law, stood up. She didn't smile; she rarely did, not even at her little granddaughter. There was a lot of tension and unpleasant history between her and James.

'She's asleep,' Paula said as she walked past him and out of the front door.

He hated asking the woman for help, but he couldn't

afford a babysitter and he had to work. If his witch of an ex-wife hadn't let him down at the last minute, he wouldn't have had the problem. To her credit, Paula never said no. James suspected she wasn't any happier with her daughter's lack of reason and responsibility than he was.

James dropped onto the worn sofa; he was hungry and thirsty, but too knackered to go to the kitchen in search of food. He closed his eyes.

11

CHAPTER ELEVEN

Matt stood at the bar, wondering for the hundredth time what he was doing. He'd scrubbed up well, even got himself a quick last-minute haircut, ordered a mineral water and was sitting watching the door. Avoiding looking at his watch or looking at the clock on the wall behind the bar, he didn't have to see the time to know she was late. She wouldn't show, and who could blame her. Thinking that the inevitable had finally happened, and he had gone completely insane. What was he playing at? Looking down at his left hand and glancing around quickly to make sure nobody was watching him, he tugged his wedding off his finger and dropped it into his pocket.

Andrew Martin walked into the bar and they exchanged a brief look before the man went to the opposite end of the bar and out of view. Matt took a deep breath, followed by a long slug of his water. Just as he decided it was time to leave, she came through the door.

She had changed from the smart suit she was wearing earlier into jeans and a top. She looked amazing, and he knew he wasn't the only man in the room who thought so. It wasn't just the way she looked that made her stand out. She had a presence. If she was an actress, they would describe it as charisma. That indefinable something that makes everyone aware of your presence in the room.

Buying her a drink, he led her to an empty table in a quieter corner of the bar. It all felt a little awkward, but they soon started chatting.

'So what brings you to Bidbury? Most people try to get away; you must have an excellent reason for moving here by choice.'

'It's not that bad, is it?'

'I'm not known for my exaggeration.' Matt said smiling at her, 'if anything I'm understating the case.'

'It's a work relocation.'

'Really?' Not believing anyone would choose Bidbury for its charm alone. 'So what do you do?'

'You could say I'm a community consultant.'

Matt looked at her blankly.

'I help people,' she said, smiling at him.

Still failing to discover anything more about her job, he was happy enough to be sitting opposite her and actually to be seen with her. 'So you'll be around for a while?'

She shrugged her shoulders in a 'maybe' type way and sipped her red wine. 'What about you?' She said. 'Did you always want to be a police officer?'

'No. Actually, I set out on the path to being a doctor. My father was a surgeon, a heart specialist. I always thought it was a noble profession, saving lives and all that.'

'What went wrong?' she asked. 'It's a bit of a leap, isn't it? I mean doctor to detective inspector.'

Matt finished his beer. He knew she was watching him closely; he felt uncomfortable and wanted desperately to

Chapter 11

believe it was because she found him fascinating and irresistible, but he had the feeling it was more like she was wondering what the hell she was doing having a drink with someone like him. 'I guess I just realised that I wasn't noble enough,' he finally said. He stood up and pointed to her barely touched glass. 'Another?'

Liz shook her head, 'no thanks.'

He got another beer for himself and returned to the table. He tried to glean more information about her and they chatted on for another twenty minutes; she was easy to talk to. But at some point he realised that she had given nothing away, or at least nothing personal about herself. His attempts to learn more about her avoided with the skill of a politician being interviewed. All he knew was that she had a daughter at University and that she'd only moved into Bidbury four days ago. So much for his interrogation skills!

It disappointed Matt when she stood up to leave, even though he had been expecting it from the moment she'd arrived. He walked her out into the street. They hovered just outside; he wasn't sure what to do next. He took a deep breath to gather his courage. Was he going to kiss her? Or ask her out again? Before he had decided, she spoke.

'So why did you do it?'

'Do what?'

'Take the ring off.'

Matt felt surprised and embarrassed. 'Am I that transparent?'

Liz took his hand. She led him towards a lamppost and she pointed to his finger. 'See the line.'

Matt shook his head. Making a total pratt of himself had not been top of his intentions for the evening. 'I thought I was the detective.'

CHAPTER ELEVEN

'So what is it? Your wife doesn't understand you?' Liz replied sarcastically.

'God, I'm a walking cliché. Would it help if I said I've never done this before?'

Liz leant forward and kissed his cheek. 'Thanks for the drink.'

He watched her walk away. 'Take that as a no then...'

Gutted, Matt headed off in the opposite direction.

CHAPTER TWELVE

For the first time, I felt a tiny stirring of compassion. I suppose it was hard not to be moved. The man didn't live well. His house was ill kept, and he had little to show for his life. A job I knew he hated, a house that wasn't a home. I could describe him as pitiful. Yet he wasn't without redemption. The shining light of his house and his life was clearly his daughter. I knew she was five, and her name was Annie. And I knew that her mother had walked out. Run off with a fitness instructor, lured by his biceps and the money he earned from private clients.

Images of the little girl made me weak, the photo beside his bed, with her huge innocent eyes staring back at me. It wasn't the tears that were streaming down his face. It wasn't his sobs or his pleading eyes. I could harden my heart to him I only had to remember what he had done. Then I could remember why I was standing in front of him pointing a gun at his head. I was calm, and the gun was steady, I knew I could, and I would pull the trigger.

He was on his knees. He was trying to write on the

CHAPTER TWELVE

carpet. It was threadbare and grubby, and he was shaking violently. He kept pleading over and over, 'no, no, no...'

He got to the second 'R' when suddenly the door opened and five-year-old Annie walked sleepily into the room, rubbing her eyes.

I couldn't have been more shocked if the police had suddenly burst in. The little girl should be at her mother's house that night. My research was meticulous.

Annie looked from her father to me, confusion and fear snuffing out her innocence.

I looked at the little girl, then down at the man. He reached out and grabbed his daughter, pushing her behind him. My finger tightened on the trigger. I was there to do a job, I couldn't fail at my task. I had to complete the execution.

13

CHAPTER THIRTEEN

Matt walked into the house.

Jen was already there. She looked up at him as he entered the lounge. 'Same format Gov, gun, lipstick, no break-in...' she glanced towards the sofa, 'just a different outcome.'

Matt looked at James. The man was sitting on his shabby sofa, with his little girl asleep, her head resting on his lap.

'You're a very lucky man,' Matt said with feeling.

A pale and haunted James stroked his young daughter's hair, 'Annie walked in and the gunman ran,' his voice was thick with emotion. 'If my baby hadn't needed a drink, I'd be a big mess on the floor right now.' He swallowed hard, fighting back tears.

Matt sat himself down on a worn out chair opposite James. But it was Jen who spoke from behind him.

'You a drug user, Mr Tate?'

Matt glanced behind him with some irritation.

'No!' James said, shocked.

'Ever dealt?'

CHAPTER THIRTEEN

'No. Never. I wouldn't. I've got a kid.' James looked at Matt. 'You know I wouldn't.'

Matt put a hand up to silence Jen. She opened her mouth to protest, but then thought better of it. Matt had been told, mainly by his wife, that he sometimes had an icy glint in his eyes. She'd said, rather nastily, that as the eyes were the window to the soul, it showed his true self. Cold and emotionless. Maybe she was right. Whatever the reason, Jen stopped talking.

Matt looked at James. The strain showed on the other man's face. He looked old, much older than Matt knew him to be. Worn out, faded, like a garment thrown through the washing cycle too many times. James had been a good-looking youth, cheeky and charming, though always shy and easily led. James looked like a man who had failed in life. Or maybe it was James who had failed to live. Either way, Matt wondered if it could all have been very different.

'Anything to help us identify the gunman?' Matt asked, pulling himself back under control.

'Person Gov.'

'What?'

'Gun person Gov.'

Matt ignored her and looked at James, who shook his head.

'He didn't speak. Not a word. All in black, balaclava left little on show. I was too shit scared to work out the colour of his eyes.'

'Height? Build?' Jen asked.

James shrugged. 'Dunno.' He looked at her, 'maybe a couple of inches taller than you.'

Matt turned his head to look at her, a question in his eyes.

Chapter 13

'Five seven,' she said. 'So we're looking at around five nine or ten.'

Matt stood up. 'Was there anything about the gun...' he glanced at Jen '... person, that you felt was familiar?'

James frowned, like he couldn't comprehend the question. 'Familiar?'

'Anyone you might have pissed off?' Jen said.

'Someone you know. Or maybe someone you used to know...' Matt said.

James paled. The colour drained away from his face, like someone had pulled a plug and drained his arteries. He looked at Matt, long and hard, and shook his head repeatedly, almost violently in denial. 'No.'

Matt followed Jen to the door. A very frightened James called after them. 'Will he be back?'

Matt kept walking. He didn't know the answer. He certainly thought it was possible, but he didn't want to share it. James felt scared enough already. 'Change your locks,' he called over his shoulder.

Outside, Matt inhaled deeply. 'Bloody lucky to be alive.'

Jen nodded her agreement, but her mind was on other matters. 'How do you know him, Gov?'

Matt paused. He wasn't ready to face up to the past that linked them all together, not yet. Preferably never.

'I mean, he talked to you like you were old mates, like you knew him well...'

Matt thought about lying. Saying that James had given him parking tickets a few times. But he wasn't a fan of lies. Besides, he knew he wasn't clever enough to maintain them. And he knew Jen well enough to know that if she smelt deception, she'd be like a rat up a drainpipe. She wouldn't let it drop.

CHAPTER THIRTEEN

'No, not mates, never mates. But we were at school together about a million years ago.'

Jen absorbed the information. 'But...'

Matt unlocked his car door. The first stirrings of morning light were trying to find a path through the clouds. It was going to be another grey day. 'There is no but Jen. This is a small town and I have lived here my entire life. James and I were at school together, that's all.'

He climbed into his car and started the engine. If only it were true, if only that really was all it was. The voice locked behind a door in his head was hammering so hard to be heard that the pain made him feel physically sick. He did what he had always done. Ignored the voice and carried on.

He looked out of his car window; James was standing by the door, staring out. A couple of uniform officers arrived to start the house to house and Jen was issuing instructions to them. Matt pulled away as one of the police officers turned to glance in his direction. He was so shocked his foot hit the accelerator instead of the brake and he slammed into the back of Jen's parked car.

Jen and the two uniformed officers hurried towards him. He turned off the engine and climbed out of his car.

'What the hell happened?' Jen shrieked.

Matt ignored her and stared at the female police officer. 'Hello...' he said.

'Made a bit of a mess,' Liz said, pointing at Jen's car.

It was a red VW Beetle, all shiny and loved. Different to his battered old black Beemer, that was well past its glossy glory days.

'You think?' Jen's nose was an inch away from the paintwork, studying the damage.

Matt looked at Liz and lowered his voice, 'Community consultant?'

Chapter 13

Liz shrugged her shoulders. 'As good a title as any. I told you I help people.'

'You didn't help me,' he said glancing at Jen's car. 'You should have told me you were a policewoman.' He kept his voice lowered; he didn't want Jen to overhear.

'You should have told me you had a wife,' she replied.

Matt couldn't argue that point, although he wanted to. He watched her as she walked away. He'd never had a thing for uniforms, but she certainly looked good in hers.

Jen stood up. 'The damage is only cosmetic,' she said, 'we'll sort insurance details out back at the station later.'

'Sure,' he replied. 'Sorry Jen.'

He climbed back into his car and drove away. He mentally replayed every word he had exchanged with Liz and knew that although she hadn't been very forthcoming with her personal information, she hadn't misled him. It was while he was remembering the previous night's encounter at the car park he remembered seeing the argument between Andrew and James. He did a U-turn in the road and headed into town.

Matt walked into the shoe shop. There were no customers, the store had only just opened, and Gemma was dusting the racks and looked up and smiled at him, 'can I help you?'

Matt nodded in her direction and headed straight for the back of the store to an open door with a STAFF ONLY sign.

'Hey you can't go through there.' The junior assistant said.

Andrew appeared in the doorway; he was clearly suffering the aftereffects of overindulgence and was cradling a still fizzing mug of Alka Seltzer. He seemed more annoyed than surprised to see Matt and stepped aside to let him into

CHAPTER THIRTEEN

the back area that served as a stockroom and staff sanctuary. 'What do you want?' He said closing the door firmly on Gemma's curiosity.

The two men stared at each other in open animosity. Andrew caved in first and moved to the kettle to fill it with water and then switch it on. 'Coffee?'

'No.'

'What then?'

'James Tate had a gun at his head last night.'

Andrew paused, a teaspoon of instant coffee in his hand. 'Dead?'

'No. He got lucky. Where were you last night?'

Andrew put the spoon of coffee in a mug; he added boiling water and stirred. 'You're kidding, right?'

'I saw you with him at the car park, you pushed him.'

'Misunderstanding. The dick wrote me a ticket. You know what he's like.'

Matt moved across the room so that he was very close to the other man. 'I know what you're like.'

Andrew held his ground. 'Why would I kill James? I'm not the one with the hang-ups from the past. If you're looking for someone with a motive, look in the mirror.'

Matt grabbed him by his shirt and slammed him up against the wall. The hot coffee splattered everywhere.

Andrew cried out as the burning liquid scolded him. 'Shit! I was at Blades, the Nightclub, you can check...'

'Oh, I will,' Matt said, stepping back.

They stared at each other briefly before Matt turned and walked out.

BACK AT HOME, Matt made himself a coffee and sat in the kitchen while he drank it. He turned the TV on and then

Chapter 13

turned it off again. Day time shows should come with a health warning. But then the alternative was silence, and he didn't like that much either.

He finished the coffee and headed upstairs. He needed to shower and change before going into the station. An image of Annie came unbidden into his mind, an innocent little girl who stood so close to tragedy. Why had the killer run off? A killer with a conscience? It could so easily have been two bodies bleeding onto James threadbare carpet.

Matt reached his bedroom and stripped down to his boxers. Barefoot and dishevelled, he headed for the bathroom. The door opened as he reached it and Avril came out. She was immaculate, dressed, made up and staring at him with ill-concealed disdain.

'Been drinking?' it was more of a statement than a question.

'No. Working.'

She gave him that; I don't believe you and don't care anyway look as she walked past him. He assumed she was going to work, although he wasn't sure he could assume anything with her anymore.

Damp from the shower, and with a towel wrapped around his waist, Matt cleaned his teeth. He never was a morning person. His electric toothbrush made a strange whirring sound before it died. With a mouthful of toothpaste and a shortage of patience, he pulled out a pack of batteries from the cabinet. He took the last two out and dropped the packaging into the bin. He missed. Even more irritated, he bent down to pick it up and tried again.

Something caught his eye. He rummaged in the bin and pulled out a spent pregnancy testing stick. The reading was negative. Matt stared at it briefly before chucking it back in with the rubbish. Irritation turned to fury. He spun round and punched the door. It seemed to represent the failure of their marriage. He was relieved and not surprised; they had only managed sex once in the past two months and that was; he was sure, just a guilt shag for his birthday! The marriage was over and a positive pregnancy test now would be a disaster.

14

CHAPTER FOURTEEN

Two murders and an attempted murder all in little over a week was a major situation in a small town like Bidbury. The offices of the local paper were in an excited frenzy. Last week's front page was a councillor caught with his fingers in the till, and that had been one of the better lead stories. Jeff, the editor, had thought it was a gift from the gods when one of his reporters uncovered the scandal. He couldn't quite believe what was happening now. He knew that this was big enough to attract national interest, and he fought to make sure that the Bidbury Herald led the way. A serial killer in his backyard, a provincial editor could wait a lifetime and never get such a lucky break. He sipped his coffee while he waited impatiently; he clicked his pen compulsively and kept his eye on the door.

When it finally opened, he jumped with excitement and spilt the coffee, splattering it down his shirt. 'What have we got?'

The man who entered was young, mid-twenties at most. Jeff liked them young. They were eager, and they took risks, dug deeper and crossed lines. They put ambition before

CHAPTER FOURTEEN

caution and often viewed morality as a movable object, easily pushed out of the way when required.

Jeff dabbed at his shirt without looking at what he was doing. His eyes kept fixed on Dan.

Dan grinned and crossed the room to the desk. 'Two dead, third one should have been. Same killer, single shot in the head...'

That didn't impress Jeff. 'Now tell me something I don't know.'

Dan waved a piece of paper at his boss. 'I have the name and address of the lucky bastard who survived the encounter.'

'Fucking fantastic,' Jeff said excitedly. He took the paper and glanced at the name, then handed it back. 'You waiting for an invitation?'

Dan hurried to the door. Jeff called after him. 'Dare I ask how?'

Dan turned around and shook his head and grinned. 'Best not to, Boss.'

Jeff watched him leave. Then he switched his computer on and did some research of his own.

They had set an incident room up, and details of the victims were pinned on the boards. A small team of detectives was waiting when Matt walked in. Jen was standing at the front of the room and glanced up at the clock as he walked towards her. He felt a surge of anger but contained it. She was right; he was late. Only two minutes, but a keen, dedicated detective should be a leader and one step ahead of the team. Like her.

Matt reached the front and got straight into it. 'James Tate is a very lucky man. This killer, until now, has been

Chapter 14

ruthless and meticulous. No sign of a break in again. We need to check who has keys, past and present. Employees, cleaners...'

'Something links these men together.' Jen said, interrupting. 'Check out their past. What schools they went to, what clubs they belonged to, who they dated. We need a motive. Who would want them dead and why?'

Jen glanced across at Matt. He forced himself to stay calm and in control. He nodded his agreement.

'Send someone to talk to his ex-wife and boyfriend, check they have alibis. We had anything back from forensics on the lipstick?' He asked.

'Not a full report. But I made a call first thing to chase it. Don't think we'll get anything from that. It's a cheap over-the-counter brand, and the colour is old, obsolete now.' She said.

'So who would buy or wear it?'

'Well, it's cheap, so maybe a teenager, although the shade is not an in colour. Maybe a prostitute or someone older with a stash of unused lipsticks.'

'I suppose you can buy job lots of old stock on eBay,' He said. 'Check it out, there must be a trail somewhere, there always is, you just have to find the breadcrumbs.'

'I'll get the tech guys looking into it for me,' Jen said.

Matt walked away. He felt like a dinosaur beside her young, excited ambition. It was an uncomfortable feeling; she was the next generation, and he was facing extinction.

He headed for Blades to check out Andrew's alibi, but it was all locked up, he'd have to return later. He looked at his watch; it was just gone one, and he wondered if Avril was due a lunch break. She worked at 'Angels' a recruitment company specialising in temporary staff and it was just around the corner from where he was standing. He

CHAPTER FOURTEEN

decided that meeting her at work might offer more neutral territory.

Matt walked into the open plan office and looked across at the desk in the far left-hand corner. A young man was sitting there, head down at the computer monitor. Confused, he glanced around the room at the other desks; they were all occupied, but not by Avril.

'Take a seat, I'll be with you in a minute...' a young smartly dressed girl said to him.

'I'm looking for Avril Mardell,' he replied, declining her invitation to sit or to wait. The girl glanced up at him with a slightly annoyed frown that quickly changed to surprise when he flashed his warrant card at her.

'I'm sorry, but she's not here.'

'I can see that. When will she be back?'

Curiosity alight in her eyes, she stared back at him, 'sorry but she doesn't work here anymore.'

'Of course she does.'

'No, she left last month.'

'Left?'

'Well, sacked really, she was always late and sometimes smelt of alcohol...' she leaned closer, 'even thought she might have got stoned sometimes...'

'Avril Mardell?' he couldn't actually believe the young girl was talking about his wife. How could she get sacked and him not know? Where was she every day?

'What's she done? Is she in trouble? I never liked her; she was always bitchy to me...'

Matt walked away. He paused at the door. 'Don't suppose you know where she's working now?'

The girl shook her head.

Another woman from the desk beside her looked across

Chapter 14

at him. 'I saw her in the estate agents at the bottom of the high street last week.'

'Working there?'

'Don't know, she had a suit on and was chatting to someone. You know the agents I mean? Can't think what it's called...'

He knew exactly which agency she meant and who it was owned by. Matt walked out of the building. He felt a bit like a rabbit caught in headlights, frozen by confusion. What he'd just heard seemed incomprehensible. He half hoped that she was working at the estate agents, even though he didn't want her to have any dealing with the owner. There was surely only one other reason she would be in the offices. He didn't fancy getting home one day to find they had sold it behind his back. He was thinking nonsense, of course, but after what he'd just been told he wasn't sure of anything.

He considered going to the estate agents in search of answers, but he no longer felt ready for the questions and confrontation that would follow, instead he returned to his car.

Matt parked outside James' house. The street was empty. Until that moment he hadn't even realised that he was hoping to see Liz, but the police and the Socos had finished with the crime scene. Matt hoped maybe they would get lucky with this one and the killer would have left a nice juicy clue for them.

He was getting pressure from above and the press were chasing for more information. His boss was making noises about getting some fancy profiler in to help. That was the last thing Matt needed. Luckily, he knew his boss well

CHAPTER FOURTEEN

enough to know that procrastination and budget trimming were his favourite past-times.

'You changed the lock?' Matt said as he followed James into the kitchen. James was in much the same state as he had been the previous night. He hadn't changed or shaved. Matt guessed he hadn't washed or showered either. A wreck of a man.

James nodded his head.

'Good.'

'Coffee?'

'No, I'm ok thanks,' Matt replied.

James switched the kettle off and pulled a bottle of whisky from a cupboard. He held it up, Matt reluctantly shook his head. James poured himself a large glass and drank it down in one go. 'Annie's with her mum,' he said even though Matt hadn't asked.

'I got your text,' Matt said. 'You wanted to see me.'

James nodded his head slowly and poured himself another drink. He looked how Matt felt. Agitated, nervous, worried. Matt just hoped he was doing a better job at hiding it.

'I always knew this day would come,' James said, staring at the bottle as though it held all the answers.

Matt certainly knew how that felt.

'I mean, we had to pay in the end, didn't we?'

Matt looked at James. Was he right? Did the past always have to be paid for? Matt had spent his adult life trying to deny the past. He had the memories locked away while he worked hard to rid the streets of the bad guys. Well, he used to work hard, and he knew his job was his pathetic attempt to redeem himself.

It terrified James, and with good reason. The man had a child to think about and protect. If he wasn't there, the poor

Chapter 14

little girl would have to live with her mother. Matt knew Lindsey well; he'd picked her up for soliciting once or twice. Pretty sure James was unaware of that. The woman was a terrible role model for their little girl, who would have a pretty rough life without her father to love and support her.

Matt knew that feeding the man's fear would serve no positive purpose. 'You're talking rubbish, mate,' he said with far more confidence than he felt. 'This is some nutter with a lipstick fetish.'

James looked doubtful. 'Really?'

'Yeah, sure. We'll soon catch the bastard.' He paused and looked at James. 'Talking of bastards, what were you and Andrew arguing about yesterday? I saw him push you...'

James rolled his eyes. 'He thinks rules don't apply to him. He was pissed at me because his permit was out of date and I gave him a parking ticket.'

'That's it? Did he threaten you?'

'Only the usual, he's a fucking bully, always has been. Why?'

Matt looked at James and decided not to push him any further. He stood up to leave, 'just watching him, that's all.'

James followed Matt to the front door. 'Had someone banging on the door earlier...'

Matt turned and looked at James.

'From the Herald. Reporter...'

'You didn't?'

'Nah, of course not, but he stuck a card through the door.' James fidgeted, his eyes dropped away from Matt and he focused on his shoes.

'What?'

'Offered me money, lots of it for an exclusive, even more for a picture of me and Annie.'

Matt understood the temptation. You only had to look

CHAPTER FOURTEEN

around the house to know the budget James had to work with. 'Not yet,' he said eventually.

As he walked away, he wondered how the reporter knew about James. They had given no update to the press yet. He knew Jeff, the editor at the Herald, had a bit of a reputation for getting whatever information he needed. Matt didn't like the idea that one of his team might be talking.

He drove back to the station, parked up and looked around, hoping to see Liz. But she was so elusive he was thinking he'd imagined seeing her in uniform at the crime scene.

LIZ CHANGED out of her uniform and left the station. The street was busy as the shops closed and workers headed home. Despite the early evening sun, she shivered; it had been a long day. Her head turned and her eyes stopped at the shoe shop. It was closed, the lights off, the shutters down.

Liz hurried on down the street, head down, keen to get home and totally lost in her own thoughts. Almost at her car, a hand reached out to touch her. She jumped. It was Matt.

'Penny for them.' He said, smiling.

He had a pleasant smile, interesting. But it never quite reached his eyes. The lips curved, the cheeks dimpled, the eyes crinkled, but somewhere in the blue depths, shadows lingered.

'Don't think a penny would get close to paying for my thoughts.' She said, wondering why she was talking to him. She knew she should ignore him, hurry to her car and head home without a backward glance.

'No? You exact a high price?'

Chapter 14

'Always.'

They stood staring at each other, Liz watched as he fidgeted slightly awkwardly. There was something about him that made her want to stay and talk. She told herself it was curiosity. But it was more than that.

'Are you following me?' she said, smiling even though she really didn't want to.

'Yes.' Matt replied, looking flustered, 'or at least I was hoping I might catch you...'

'Catch me what?' she said teasingly.

'Off guard, maybe? Enough to agree to have dinner with me?'

Liz shook her head and walked to the car. What in the world was she playing at? She pressed the key fob to unlock her car.

But he was persistent. 'Oh, come on. Just dinner, what's the harm?'

At her car door, Liz paused. Could she? Dare she? 'You're married...'

'I'm not offering you a night of passionate sex, just a bite to eat.'

Liz smiled, he had a certain charm that made him hard to say no to and before she could stop herself the words were out her mouth. 'In that case, how can I refuse?'

15

CHAPTER FIFTEEN

Matt looked across the table at Liz. What was he playing at? Aside from the fact that he had a killer on the loose and should work flat out to catch him, he was also still a married man. Ok, the marriage was in tatters, but was that really an excuse? Liz was a very attractive woman; he was delusional if he really believed he only wanted dinner.

He watched as Liz looked around the restaurant. It was full of eighties memorabilia. Hits from the era played in the background and photos decorated the walls.

'Cheesy isn't it?' he asked, wishing he'd chosen somewhere more classy and sophisticated. Not that many such places existed in Bidbury. But he could have taken her to the little Italian Bistro or the restaurant in the posh hotel at the edge of town.

'Yep, very...' Liz grinned 'but I love it.'

'Really?' did she mean it or was she being polite, or worse just humouring him through some misplaced pity. He was pretty sure he had a luminous L for loser on his forehead.

Chapter 15

He watched as her eyes paused at one photo. A couple of girls dressed in short RaRa skirts, with high heels and big hair. A fleeting sadness touched her eyes, quickly hidden but not fast enough for Matt to miss. 'What is it?' he said, concerned.

Liz shook her head and smiled. 'I was just reflecting on the fact that I had a skirt just like that. Embarrassing or what!'

'And the hair?'

'Oh yes, especially the hair...' she showed with her hands just how big the hair had been.

Matt laughed. 'Dare I admit to having a mullet?'

'Very cool.'

'Yep, that was me.'

The server approached them and they both ordered burgers. Matt looked across the table at her and realised that he was laughing for the first time in weeks, maybe even months, possibly even years. He lent forward, 'so what did you and your big hair dream of? What did you want to be or do?'

'Well, I wanted to be in a girl band, but I couldn't sing...'

'Hmm, slight problem, but not insurmountable.'

'But I couldn't dance either,' she said.

'So you couldn't sing or dance, not the best way into a band. So what was your back-up plan?'

'To marry George Michael!'

'Oh dear...'

In the background the Wham song 'Wake me up before you go, go...' played. Matt looked at her and she giggled. The server brought their burgers, and he grinned at her, feeling as a giddy as a schoolboy on his first date.

. . .

CHAPTER FIFTEEN

Andrew was on the dance floor. He thought he was John Travolta, but actually he was just a drunk stumbling mess. He thought he was dancing with a couple of attractive, scantily dressed young girls. But he wasn't. Every time they moved away from him, he followed.

One bouncer was watching him warily.

The girls were getting annoyed. He upped the tempo, doing his dirty dancing routine. His erratic gyrations made him lose his balance. He stumbled and fell onto one girl, grabbing her for support.

She shook him off in disgust, and he fell to the floor.

The bouncer pushed his way through the dancers.

Andrew got to his feet and swung around to face the girl who let him fall. 'Hey sweetie, that wasn't friendly.'

The girl's friend butted in. 'Piss off pervert.'

Andrew's temper flared. He raised his fist. But the bouncer was ready and grabbed him from behind. Another bouncer quickly joined the fray. They dragged Andrew away. He shouted after the girl. 'Fucking tease.'

Andrew hit the floor, hard. The bouncers did not soften the blow. He picked himself up and vomited onto the curb. He wiped his mouth on his shirt cuff and stumbled towards the road, trying to hail a cab, but the cabs wouldn't stop.

Swearing and cursing to himself, Andrew staggered home.

Matt and Liz walked away from the restaurant. Matt relaxed, the evening had gone well. They were at ease with each other; they walked close, but not touching. Her body language was open, and it encouraged him. They reached the car park and Liz reached in her handbag for her keys. She pressed the remote and Matt opened the door for her.

Chapter 15

He looked down and into her eyes and without allowing himself time to think or reflect; he leant forward and kissed her gently on the lips. She didn't pull away, at least not immediately. Her lips were soft and warm and he wanted to stay like that forever.

But after a few fleeting seconds, she stepped back.

'I know I said only dinner, but I'm open to persuasion...' he said.

Liz climbed into her car. 'Goodnight,' she said, closing the car door and firmly shutting him out.

KYLIE WAS SOUND ASLEEP. Curled up in the foetal position, the quilt pulled up high around her. The bedroom curtains were slightly open and light from the streetlamp outside flickered, casting eerie shadows.

A noise from outside and she awoke immediately, wide awake and full of fear.

Kylie could hear his footsteps on the drive, and in her head she could see him fumbling in his pocket for the door key. She heard the key in the lock and the door open and then slam shut behind him. She knew he'd see the mutt. He always did. No matter how pissed, he always petted Bruce the dog. The kitchen door closed, and she heard him start up the stairs. Heavy drunken footsteps. She knew every creak and every groan that each step made. The third from the top was the noisiest. He was almost at the landing. She heard him stumble and swear.

Kylie pulled the covers tight around her. She looked across at the door and was glad she had pushed her chest of drawers against it. A small and ineffective barrier. She knew it wouldn't stop him.

The footsteps paused right outside her door.

CHAPTER FIFTEEN

Kylie was trembling. She closed her eyes and wished herself away, anywhere, anywhere but there. If she believed in god, she would pray now. But she didn't, so she couldn't. No one could help her, not the school or the social worker who came snooping around last year, and definitely not divine intervention.

The footsteps moved on past, and Kylie breathed again.

She lay back down and listened to him heaving in the bathroom. If there really was a god or any justice in the world, then surely her father should choke on his own vomit and die.

MATT WAS ALONE in the house. Again. He wondered where his wife was. What she was doing every night until the early hours. And who she was doing it with! Then he wished he hadn't. Some thoughts were best left well alone. He picked up the full bottle of whisky that was on the table beside him. He stared at it for several seconds and then with some reluctance and a surge of resolve he put it down and took himself off to bed.

But he couldn't sleep. The demons that had haunted him for twenty years had gone into overdrive. Like a child who had feasted on cola and cake, his demons were hyperactive and wouldn't give him any peace. He sat up and without turning on the light he pulled a bottle of pills from his drawer. He took two out and headed for the bathroom to get some water to take them.

Back in bed, he lay down and waited for sleep.

But even with the tablets, it eluded him. He climbed out of bed and went downstairs. The whisky was where he'd left it. Full, unopened, and taunting him with his weakness. He poured himself a large glass and drank it down in one go.

Chapter 15

Then, cradling the bottle and the glass, he headed back upstairs to his bedroom. He paused in the doorway and thought he heard a noise. Was Avril home? He walked across the room and glanced at the bedside clock. Two am. How had his marriage come to this?

Matt sat down on the bed and poured another glass. He drank it swiftly. Then he stood up and walked to the window. He looked out and down to the drive. His wife's car wasn't there. Maybe she'd got a taxi home.

A noise behind him made him spin around and all his nightmares suddenly became reality.

The figure was all in black. His fear heightened and Matt half wished he'd put a light on so at least he could see his killer properly. But maybe it was better this way. Resignation washed over him. He wished he hadn't had the whisky. He could feel its warmth surging through his veins, making him slow and sleepy. Matt's eyes focused on the gun pointed at his head. The gloved hand that held it was steady.

Matt thought about fighting. He imagined himself lunging for the killer and wrestling the gun from his hand. But even with his brain as slow as it was, he knew he would be dead before he'd even made the first step. It seemed the sleeping tablets were finally kicking in. His eyelids were heavy, and the world was spinning.

The gunman was waving at him to get on his knees. Just as well as he was pretty sure he was about to fall down, anyway.

Matt knew he should be afraid, and he was, but probably not as much as he ought to be. All he really wanted to do was sleep. Even the adrenaline that was surging through his body couldn't counter the effect of sleeping pills and the whisky.

The killer lowered the gun and left the bedroom.

CHAPTER FIFTEEN

Matt couldn't comprehend what was happening. Had they had fired the gun? Was he hit? Was he dying or was he already dead?

His body collapsed onto the floor, he tried to keep his eyes open; he didn't want to die alone. He heard footsteps. The killer was back, returned to finish him. He tried to lift his head, but it was as heavy as lead. The figure leaned down and looked into his face.

Matt fought for clarity. He tried to focus. All he saw was a bleary image of his wife Avril with the look of contempt that he expected from her. His eyes closed, and he slid into darkness.

16

CHAPTER SIXTEEN

Liz walked down the high street. It was lunchtime, and the town was busy. Uniform were on a PR exercise, displaying a reassuring presence and pretending the police were in control. The public were getting twitchy with a killer on the prowl, and the press were feeding the fear. So police officers were out in force in clean shiny uniforms and she was walking through the town centre as a representative of law and order. Of course, a quicker answer could be available if all uniformed officers were hands on in the investigation. But that was police politics for you. It all came down to perception.

She didn't really mind. She would rather walk around and mingle rather than be at a desk piled with paperwork or more house to house questioning. Her head was all over the place. She'd struggled all morning to get focused and motivated. If she were in the mood for being honest, she would have to admit that the reason for her distraction was Matt. But she wasn't ready for honesty and was pretending not to think about him at all.

A shopper approached and Liz looked up with a smile

ready on her lips. The smile faltered. It was an elderly lady, smartly dressed and fully made up. She had clearly been a stunner once, but now looked faded with an air or resignation and sadness.

The lady looked at Liz. 'Hello Beth.'

Liz took a deep breath. She knew that this meeting would come. She thought she had prepared for it; but she was wrong. 'What are you doing here?'

'I could ask you the same thing?'

'I'm working...' All Liz really wanted to do was run. Get out; get away, as far away as possible. Moving back to the town inevitably meant that her mother would hear about it. The WI had spies everywhere and her mother was queen of the cupcakes. But seeing her mother standing in front of her was tough. The pain and the anger was as raw and powerful now as it had always been. Time did not heal. That was a myth. Time just masked the emotions.

'I can see that. Can you take a break? We could have a coffee.'

'Just go,' Liz said, desperately trying to keep a grip on her emotions. She didn't want to create a scene.

'That's it? You can't be civil to your own mother?' The lady reached out to touch her arm, 'please Beth...'

Liz looked into her mother's eyes. She could see the pain and sorrow of loss and separation. The eyes were a watery grey; they used to be clear and blue like a summer's day. A tiny slither of sympathy and regret stirred. She shook it away along with her mother's arm.

'I'm busy,' she said and hurried away.

Andrew paced the shop floor. Bored and restless was an understatement. There was only one customer in the shop.

An elderly man, Gemma could handle him. Without bothering to tell Gemma, he left the shop. He headed down the high street towards the pub. He crossed the road and as he did so he saw Liz. There was something vaguely familiar about her. She was a stunner alright, certainly memorable. He wondered if she'd arrested him, which had happened a few times, unfairly to his mind, when all he'd done was to enjoy a few drinks. Either that or he'd seen her around.

She looked his way and their eyes locked and held. Just briefly, before she turned and walked further into the shadows, away from his view.

Andrew felt unsettled by the brief encounter. He couldn't account for it. He definitely needed a drink.

The first thought that struck Matt was that he was alive. The second was that he felt like shit. He was on the floor and he ached all over, which was bad enough, but nothing compared to the searing pain in his head when he tried to sit up. Looking down at his body; he was only wearing boxer shorts, easy to check for bullet holes or dried blood.

What the hell had happened last night?

According to his clock it was lunchtime, he'd be late for work, although that seemed to be the least of his problems. He picked up the bottle of pills and read the label. Big letters: Do Not Drink Alcohol...

Bugger, bit late for the information check now, he probably should have read the label before taking them. The doctor had prescribed them months ago, maybe even as long as a year ago. Insomnia had been his constant companion for years, but the doctor thought that his inability to impregnate his wife must be down to stress and lifestyle. He suggested gentle exercise, healthy diet, meditation, massage and sleeping pills. Of course, the best route to pregnancy was sex. But they had both given up on that weeks ago. And even before that it had become sporadic, and only when Avril's fertility charts dictated.

Avril? He needed to remember something about her. He had an image of her face looking down at him. She had been there last night; he was sure it was her.

Matt stumbled from the bedroom. He was still groggy, the hangover from hell. He pulled open the door to the spare room, but it was empty so he forced himself to tackle the stairs even though every step jarred his body and sent a shooting pain into his head.

But Avril was not in the house.

He made himself a coffee and searched the kitchen drawers until he found a box of paracetamol. He sank down into a chair at the table and tried to relive and remember the previous night's events. With little success. His thoughts had become blurred and unfocused. Had he imagined the whole thing? Surely if the killer had been in his house, in his bedroom, pointing a gun at him, he would not be sipping coffee several hours later.

By the time he got showered, dressed and at his desk at work, Matt had convinced himself that none of it was real.

17

CHAPTER SEVENTEEN`

It had been a long and difficult shift. Liz parked her car on the drive and climbed out. Seeing her mother had really rattled her, and she hadn't been able to concentrate all day. The only good thing was that focusing on her mother meant she'd been able to block Matt from her thoughts. How had everything become so confused?

Her neighbours were in the front garden. Liz had mostly avoided them, although they spent a lot of their time outside. Since it was already immaculate, Liz had concluded they liked to watch the street life unfurling. The man was middle-aged and wore a long suffering expression; he was mowing a lawn that didn't need mowing. His wife was weeding, or at least was pretending to be engaged in the task while spying on the street life.

The woman waved, and Liz smiled and waved back, desperately hoping that she wouldn't have to stop and talk. All she wanted was a strong cup of tea and a long soak in a hot bath.

The young teenage daughter of the couple hurried out

of the house. She was dressed for some fun – short skirt, skimpy top, bare midriff, hair newly straightened and her face made up. She was a pretty girl with a wide sunny smile.

Her mother did not however share the smile. Liz watched as the woman stood up and scowled at her daughter.

'You can't go out looking like that. You're asking for trouble...'

The teenager's smile disappeared.

A car with windows down, music pumping, pulled up. The daughter ran for the car, climbed in, and it they shot off at speed.

MEMORIES SUDDENLY CAME FLOODING BACK to Liz. She was fifteen, her sister Melissa two years older. They dressed to impress. Just like in the pictures on the wall at the place she had dinner with Matt, short RaRa skirts, big, big hair, high heels and great glittery makeup. Liz had been proud of the look, Mary Quant; she'd spent all her Saturday job wages from Woolworths on buying it. They were laughing and joking together, happy and excited, until their mother followed them out of the house wagging her finger.

'You look like a pair of cheap tarts. Don't come crying to me when you get into trouble.'

LIZ GRITTED her teeth against the unwanted memory and watched the car drive away. She walked across to the fence and looked directly at the woman.

'Nobody asks for trouble, but sometimes it finds you, anyway,' she said. Without waiting for an answer she turned around and headed quickly for her front door.

Chapter 17

Once safely inside, she couldn't hold the tears back any longer.

Matt, her mother, memories. It was all too much.

18

CHAPTER EIGHTEEN

I knew this hit would be successful. No more mistakes. I had to up the pace; I was already behind schedule. And now I had the added problem of dealing with James Tate. Getting close to him a second time wouldn't be easy. I had been weak. But I knew what I had to do, and nothing was going to stop me.

I would leave him to be the last. Or maybe second to last. Let him get complacent, catch him with his guard down. Right now I had to concentrate on this job.

The house was dark. That suited me fine, I knew the layout; I had memorised it. The street was quiet, a nice suburban house with neatly trimmed hedges and perfect lawns. Brian Chard had done very well for himself. I knew he had divorced; he had a daughter who lived with his ex, and he ran a small but profitable estate agency. He'd remained independent, mainly because he'd cornered the lucrative lettings market. Even now, with house prices plummeting and the recession biting, he was doing alright.

I'd watched him closely and frequently for several years. He was a charmer. Always ready with a smile and a hand-

Chapter 18

shake. The man who made everyone his best mate. I'd had to stop myself a few times from running over and declaring to the world that the man was a fake. Why could nobody look into his eyes and see the blackness that dwelled within? Strip away the trappings of success and charm and all that's left is bleak, black evil.

I had three names on my hit list that were highlighted in red. Thick, bright blood red, and he was the first of them. I'd known, even in the moment of my deepest terror and torment, that he was different. Him and the other two. When all around were doing dreadful deeds, he stood out as a man motivated by cruelty and hatred. A man without humanity.

As I slipped quietly into his house, I felt a surge of excitement. I knew he would want to live. I knew he would not give up his life easily.

I was right.

His eyes never stopped searching for a chance, an opportunity to escape. He offered me money and tried to cut a deal. He was babbling until the end. Anything he could think of to buy me or bribe me. The bastard even offered me his daughter.

It's always in the eyes.

Why did nobody else ever see it? Had his wife? Or was she as blind as everyone else?

Fighting back tears when resignation finally found him. He knew he was going to die. He dropped the lipstick onto the carpet and looked up at me. 'Do I get to know what I'm sorry for?' he sounded indifferent, dismissive, even though his voice broke from fear. If I hadn't hated him so much, I might have admired him for that.

I pointed the gun, and then on a whim I pulled the balaclava from my head.

I saw his shock, then surprise, as recognition was replaced by terror. He went to lunge for me, but the bullet stopped him. A perfect shot straight into the forehead.

I almost expected to see black blood ooze from him, but I knew I was being absurd.

The bastard was dead.

MATT HEARD HER COME IN. He glanced at the clock beside his bed and groaned. It was almost two when he'd heard her shoes on the stairs. He knew she wouldn't come into their bedroom. He was right. She went straight for the spare room and shut the door. How had it come to this? They had been happy once, hadn't they? He thought so, but then how and when had it all gone so wrong?

Even through the wall he could hear that she was crying. And not just a few muffled tears. She was sobbing loudly. He thought about going to her. He even threw the covers back and climbed out of bed. But then he changed his mind. She wouldn't want to see him, or talk to him. Their marriage was over, they both knew that. He couldn't comfort her. He couldn't give her any of the things she wanted. Not even a baby. He tried to switch his mind off and not dwell on who or what had reduced her to tears. It certainly wasn't him; the only emotion she had left for him was contempt.

Wrapping the quilt around him and pulling it up to his face to muffle the sounds of his failed marriage, he went back to sleep.

19

CHAPTER NINETEEN

Matt stared down at the body of Brian Chard. He knew he couldn't deny the link any longer. Three dead bodies, James, a near miss. He couldn't shrug it off as a coincidence.

Jen hurried into the room. She was flushed and excited. 'We've got 'em Gov...'

Matt knew her well enough not to get overwhelmed by her enthusiasm. What she probably meant was that tyre tracks from something really popular, like a Ford Fiesta had been found. That would narrow it down to about a third of Bidbury inhabitants.

'Guy across the road...' she continued, 'he runs the neighbourhood watch for the street. He has a camera pointed out of his bedroom window and straight onto this front door!'

It mildly impressed Matt. Certainly better than tyre tracks, but he had a feeling that this killer would not be so easy to track. Each hit had shown a level of competence that could only have come about after meticulous planning. Matt was pretty sure that would have included extensive

CHAPTER NINETEEN

surveillance. But he knew he ought to show some enthusiasm, so he forced himself to smile. 'Great. So what's it show then?'

Jan got very animated, barely able to contain herself. 'A figure left the house just after midnight. Looked like a woman. They got into a car and drove away at speed.'

He could tell by her face there was more. 'And?'

'And we got the registration number, Jefferson is running a check on it now.'

Matt allowed a tiny spark or optimism to stir. Maybe they would get lucky with this one. 'Good work. Anything else on the tape?'

'Not on a tape, Gov,' she said. 'It goes straight onto the laptop.'

He knew she was silently laughing at him, and probably with good reason. He felt old and obsolete and was wondering if it was time for a desk job.

PC Jefferson hurried into the doorway. He stopped without entering and waited until Matt and Jen turned around from the body to face him.

'Result?' Jen demanded.

Jefferson looked down at his notepad and read from it. 'Car belongs to a Mrs Avril Cane. The address is number 9 Chilton gardens...'

Matt reached out and snatched the notebook from the young PC. He stared at it in disbelief.

'Sir?' the young PC said uncertainly.

'Chilton gardens, why is that familiar?' Jen asked, 'Do you know her Gov?'

Matt looked up from the notebook and stared at Jen. 'She's my wife. Cane is her maiden name.'

. . .

Chapter 19

Liz groaned. Her bed was warm and comforting, her dreams had been unusually happy and it was Saturday and a rare day off. But someone was banging on her door, and whoever they were, they didn't seem to take the hint to bugger off.

With huge reluctance, Liz threw the quilt off and climbed out of bed. She stepped into her slippers and wrapped a fluffy dressing gown around her pyjamas, then she headed out of her bedroom and down the stairs.

Seriously irritated, she pulled the door open.

Dawn was standing there, one finger pressed on the bell and with her other hand waving goodbye to Phillip as he drove away. Dawn, elegant and immaculate as ever and wearing a huge beaming smile, stepped into the hallway. 'You need coffee.'

Liz was far from being impressed. 'What are you doing here? And why are you hammering on my door? It's barely morning...'

Dawn was totally unperturbed by the outburst and walked into the kitchen. 'I wasn't hammering, and it's nearly nine.'

Liz slammed the front door shut and followed her friend into the kitchen. 'You got any idea how rare it is to get an entire weekend off? I don't need you waking me up!'

Dawn let Liz rant. She calmly found her way around the kitchen; she boiled the kettle, pulled two mugs from the cupboard and found the instant coffee.

Liz sat down at the kitchen table. Dawn plonked the steaming coffee in front of her.

'Still a miserable cow in the mornings then...' Dawn said happily. 'Shut up and drink. Toast?'

Liz nodded her head and sipped the coffee.

'So what time are we leaving then?' Dawn asked as she

placed a couple of slices of hot buttery toast in front of her.

Liz took a long slurp of the coffee and waited for the caffeine to hit the spot. She looked at her friend, a combination of irritation and amazement. 'How did you know?'

Dawn shrugged her shoulders elegantly. 'I just did.'

Liz nodded her head in resignation. 'Nobody likes a smart arse, keep the coffees flowing; I'll get ready.'

M<small>ATT WISHED</small> there was another way. If only miss sunny smile and ultra-efficient Jen hadn't been standing beside him. But she was, and there was no way he could bypass procedure, not for a possible serial killer. Of course he knew it wasn't his wife. It was true that the partners of killers always claimed to be innocent of any knowledge. Sonia Sutcliffe, wife of the Yorkshire ripper, claimed she had no idea what her husband was up too. But Matt knew exactly what he was going to hear from his wife's lips, and it wasn't an admission of murder.

He wasn't allowed to question her. He had to leave that to Jen. Of all the people in the station, she was the one to grill his wife about why she was at another man's house in the middle of the night.

Matt knew why, he didn't need to be a genius or even a detective to work it out. Soon so would everyone else in the station. Most already did. He kept getting sympathy glances from colleagues. He paced the corridor, waiting. Jen came out. She didn't want to look him in the eye; he couldn't blame her for that.

'She said she was sleeping with him.' Jen said to her shoes.

'Right.' Was all he managed to reply.

'They had a fight. She left...'

Chapter 19

'What time?'

Jen did look up then, perhaps surprised at his fake matter-of-fact tone and controlled demeanour. 'Why?'

He gave her a look that reminded her that he was the senior officer and had the right to ask even though it was his wife sat inside the room.

'Just after midnight, which is verified by the neighbour's camera,' she said.

'So we need a time of death,' he replied calmly. Silently he was wondering what his wife was doing between leaving Brian Chard's house and turning up in tears at home a couple of hours later. He was confident that she would have a good explanation, well fairly confident.

'Should have it soon Gov,' she said. She fidgeted uncomfortably. 'We'll have to keep her in for a bit, and we need to search the house…' her voice trailed off, and she studied her shoes again.

It was a novelty to see her so awkward and uncomfortable. In different circumstances, he might have taken some perverse enjoyment from it.

'In case she has a stash of lipsticks and a gun in her knickers drawer?' He couldn't quite keep the bitter bite from his voice. Obviously he knew she was only doing her job, and it must be pretty difficult for her as well. Even so, he felt unreasonable hostility towards her, and for the first time he had a glimmer of understanding for all the suspects that had been angry and uncooperative. It was a disturbing feeling to be accused.

'I'll organise a search warrant.'

'No need,' he said relenting. He dug in his pocket and pulled out his house keys. 'Be my guest,' he handed them over and left the station. Was he afraid that they might find something? Of course not, he told himself firmly. But he had

CHAPTER NINETEEN

to admit he was a tiny bit worried. He couldn't shake the memory of the night he had the gun pointed at him. If it was real and not some drug, drink induced nightmare, then it had been Avril's face looking into his own.

LIZ WAS SITTING on the damp grass between two gravestones. Freshly laid flowers rested on each. Slowly she got up and walked back towards her car. Dawn was waiting patiently for her.

'Thornton's?' Dawn said. 'To hell with the diet, today we need chocolate.'

Liz drove in silence. She parked the car, and they both climbed out and headed up the high street. Inside the Chocolate shop, Liz found a free table and Dawn went to the counter to make the order. The shop was busy; it hadn't been open very long and with the recession biting hard Liz feared it might not survive.

Dawn put two glass mugs down on the table along with two chocolates.

'What is that?' Liz said, pointing to the overflowing mug.

'Hot choc with everything.'

Liz scooped up a spoonful of cream and marshmallows and found herself smiling.

'See, it's magical stuff.' Dawn said pleased.

The smile was fleeting. 'It's been two years,' Liz said.

'I know.'

'I miss him.'

'Of course you do, but it is time to move on. I know why you married him; I know it was the right thing to do. But seriously Liz don't you ever wish you could find that kind of love and passion for yourself?'

Liz wasn't upset or offended, just sad, 'well you're living

proof that love hurts.'

Dawn pulled a face. 'Ouch.'

Liz smiled gently. 'What Steve and I had was special. We supported each other, and we loved each other.'

'Yeah, I know, but as friends with separate bedrooms. Now it's time to let the past go, time you found a man of your own to love.'

An image of Matt flashed into her brain; she banished it and sipped her hot chocolate. 'Give it up, Dawn. I'm a lost cause. I'll settle for watching you dance to love's tune...'

'Ha bloody ha!'

PHILLIP STOOD at the door waiting for Dawn. Liz watched him as he was watching her friend slip into her jacket. What was the deal? Clearly he adored her, and she was utterly in love with him, so what kept them apart?

Liz hugged Dawn. 'Thanks for today.'

Dawn smiled. 'Anytime.'

Liz watched them drive away and felt very alone. Briefly she wondered what it would be like to be in love like Dawn was. She shook away the threatening melancholy and made herself a mug of tea. She looked up, surprised as she heard the front door open. The kitchen door soon followed and a smiling Sam skipped into the room.

Sam kissed Liz on the top of the head and started rummaging in the fridge. 'I'm starving.'

Liz stood up; she couldn't quite hide the worried frown. 'Alright love?'

'Of course, I just wanted to see my mum. Nothing wrong with that...'

Liz knew her daughter far too well to take that statement at face value. Something was definitely up.

20

CHAPTER TWENTY

Matt watched from the edge of the pitch. A group of men, all old enough to know better were playing a vicious game of rugby. They had replaced skill and agility with brute force and ignorance.

Amongst the losing team was Andrew.

The referee blew the whistle, and Andrew launched a tirade of offensive language towards him. The captain from the winning side joined in to support the referee, and Andrew tackled him to the ground. Matt watched as Andrews's team-mate Kevin pulled him off and dragged him towards the changing rooms.

Matt headed for the clubhouse. He ordered himself a mineral water when what he really wanted was a whisky and sat himself down to wait.

It wasn't long before Andrew and Kevin, showered and changed, reached the bar. They didn't turn and look around; they didn't see Matt. But he was close enough to hear them.

'You heard about Adam and Sharpy?' Kevin said. 'Both dead, and James was nearly a gonna.'

Chapter 20

Andrew drank his pint down in one long gulp. He tapped the empty glass down onto the surface and the barman filled it up again.

'So what? It'll be drugs; Adam always was a smack head.'

Kevin glanced across at the wall which was covered with photos, past teams and past glories. 'You don't think there's a connection?'

Andrew was more interested in his beer. 'What are you on about?'

'I read it in the paper today, big front page. It said they were executed, single shot in the head.'

Matt frowned. He hadn't seen the paper that morning. How would they have got information like that? He had ordered his team not to give out any details for fear of a copycat.

'Picture of James' kid and his slutty wife, you remember her...' Kevin demonstrated with his hands that the size of her breasts were worth remembering if nothing else about her was.

'Oh yeah, Lindsey, got off with her one night...'

Kevin didn't look convinced. Matt agreed. The woman had a lot of faults, but she had an instinctive type of intelligence that would keep her away from a man like Andrew. She went for men that she could use and manipulate; she was in many ways a female mirror image of the man. Matt was fuming that she had stolen the publicity from her ex-husband and felt guilty that he had told James not to speak to the press.

Andrew pushed another pint towards Kevin.

Kevin turned around from the bar and saw Matt. He stared at him for several seconds before he nodded a brief acknowledgement and then turned away. Matt watched as he leaned in closer to Andrew. 'All I'm saying is that maybe we ought to get ourselves a bit of protection.' Kevin pulled a pen from his jacket pocket and scribbled a number onto the back of a bar mat. He handed it to Andrew. 'Give 'em a call.'

Andrew shoved the card into his pocket and finished his third pint. 'Come on, let's get out of here,' he said.

Neither of the men looked his way again. Matt watched them leave. He still wasn't willing to let Andrew off the hook. The man was a mean bastard and Matt would love to get him locked up for something, especially if it carried a life sentence. But Andrew's alibi for the attempt on James' life almost checked out. Bouncers confirmed he had been at the nightclub, but none of them could say for certain what time he left. So the hook was still clinging to Andrews's shirt, but only just.

Matt's mobile phone rang. It was Jen. Reluctantly he picked it up, and she told him that his wife was being released. The time of death was almost two hours later than she had been seen leaving the property. The search of his house hadn't turned up a gun, and they had nothing to hold her on. Reading between the lines, he knew that there was a 'yet' that Jen would love to add to the sentence. His young colleague couldn't quite keep the edge out of her voice, it was clear that in Jen's eyes, Avril was still the number one suspect.

'You definitely don't know what time she got home?' Jen said.

'No,' he lied, 'I told you before, I took a sleeping pill...'

He didn't really know why he lied. If he was honest, he was more than a bit concerned about Avril himself. But she was still his wife and he couldn't, or wouldn't allow himself to doubt her.

Avril was already at home when he got there. She'd

ordered a taxi rather than wait for him to pick her up. He was glad; he didn't really want to be anywhere near the station. He could imagine the rumours and the gossiping. Nobody would want him around to spoil the fun. It was probably the best scandal to hit Bidbury station in years. Detective Inspector married to a serial killer. He knew the hard core gossips wouldn't let a little thing like lack of evidence get in the way of a good story. And even when they did finally let it drop everyone would know his wife was having an affair.

She was in the bedroom throwing things into a suitcase. He had expected as much, but even so it hurt, he felt like he'd been punched, hard in the gut.

'Don't try to stop me.'

He had no intentions of doing so. 'Where will you go?'

She was angry. But it was fake anger to hide her pain. He wondered if she got upset because Brian Chard was dead or because they had found her out. Had she loved the man? He wanted to ask but couldn't. Was he afraid of her answer? He didn't know. In a strange and unexpected way, seeing her pack, he felt relief. At least it was over now. No more pretending. No more clinging to empty hopes. No more trying for a baby that was never going to happen and no more looking into her eyes and seeing her disappointment and his own failings.

'I have friends,' she answered, struggling to do up the suitcase.

He squashed it down for her while she pulled the zip around. She picked the case up from the bed and they looked at each other, briefly, sadly. Then she looked away and began filling the next case.

He hovered in the doorway. He even wondered if he should offer to help, but didn't. It didn't seem right, helping your wife to pack ready to walk out on you. But watching didn't seem right either.

Obviously she felt the same way. She stopped emptying her underwear drawer into the case and looked at him. 'I loved him,' she said, tears filling her eyes. 'Sorry, but I did. I just thought you should know.'

Did it make it better or worse? He wasn't sure. The first thought that struck him was way? Brian Chard was a dick, always had been. But he kept his mouth shut.

'He made me feel special...' she continued.

He finally realised that he didn't want to hear anymore. He turned around and walked out of the room, down the stairs and out of the house.

THE GYM WAS ALMOST EMPTY. Early evening on a Saturday and people had better things to do. Not him. He was running fast on the treadmill. Sweat poured down his face and onto his chest. He turned the speed up again, faster and faster.

His mind skipped back to the Rugby club. Andrew and Kevin were on the field. They were young then and surrounded by the rest of the winning youth team. Matt was amongst them. He remembered how he'd reached out to touch the trophy before Andrew grabbed it and held it up high in a triumphant salute. Then showered and changed the entire team had gone to the clubhouse for beer, and lots of it. Nobody cared that a few of them weren't quite eighteen. They were celebrating, and this was the eighties.

LIZ WALKED into the gym and saw him immediately. She hesitated; she'd expected to be alone. He spotted her in the mirrors that covered the walls. He slowed down. She walked towards him.

'That was a serious workout.' She said taking in the rivers of sweat that stained his top.

He nodded while he waited for his breathing to return to normal.

'I wonder what you're running away from.' She said it lightly, flippantly, but his head snapped up and their eyes locked together. She stepped onto the treadmill beside him and started jogging.

MATT SPENT a long time under the shower. Then, dry and dressed, he waited outside for her. She wasn't long. He stubbed his cigarette out as soon as he saw her and smiled.

'Fancy a drink?' he asked hopefully while wondering what the hell he was doing.

'No.'

'Dinner?'

'No.'

She walked away, making him run to catch up with her.

'Sex?' in for a penny, he thought at the same time as kicking himself for being so ridiculous. What would a woman like her ever see in him?

She stopped walking and turned round, laughing. 'Still no,' she said.

He must have looked as much the pathetic loser as he felt because she seemed to take pity on him.

'Really, I can't. Not tonight.'

'Tomorrow then?' He asked, hope restored.

'Maybe,' she said before she walked away.

Matt watched her go and made his way to the pub. He finished his second pint and knew that if he didn't stop drinking right then, he wouldn't stop until he was unconscious. While he was pondering his very limited options, Andrew and Kevin entered the pub. They were already well past the stopping point, especially Andrew, who needed Kevin to support him.

Matt put his glass down and left.

L<small>IZ AND</small> S<small>AM</small> were on the Wii. Sam jumped up when the doorbell rang. 'It'll be Craig, he said he'd try to come over tonight.'

While Sam went to answer the door, Liz continued to play.

The door to the lounge opened. 'Come for a thrashing.' She said, without pausing in her actions. It was a shooting game, and she knew she could beat her daughter's young boyfriend.

But it wasn't Craig.

'I'm impressed.' Matt said from behind her.

Liz dropped the controller and span around in surprise.

Sam looked between her mother and Matt, a speculative gleam in her eyes.

Matt walked into the room and picked up the dropped controller, handing it to her. 'You're good at that.'

Liz shrugged her shoulders casually.

'I'll make some tea, shall I?' Sam said.

Liz stood up quickly. 'He's not stopping.'

'Milk, two sugars. Thanks.' Matt said grinning at Sam, who smiled back, clearly intrigued. With a quick searching glance at her mother, she left the room.

'What are you doing here?' Liz demanded, wondering why despite being annoyed there was a tiny rebellious spark of pleasure at seeing him.

Chapter 20

Matt reached out and took her hand. 'I couldn't wait until tomorrow.'

Liz snatched her hand away. 'Learn some patience. And how did you find me?'

Matt looked guilty. 'I looked your file up.'

'That's confidential!' she snapped, outraged and just a tiny bit flattered.

'I needed to see you,' he said, taking her hand again.

She didn't snatch it away immediately, even though she knew she should. She didn't want him in her house. Looking down at her; he looked deeply, searchingly into her eyes. He bent his head and kissed her gently. Fleetingly she let herself savour the moment, enjoy the feel of his lips on hers, but then she pulled back.

'Why do I feel like we've met before?'

Liz withdrew her hand and stepped right back away from him. She moved to the other side of the room and sat down. 'Because you like clichés?'

He laughed.

Sam returned with the tea. She placed the tray on the coffee table and then sat down on the sofa. She patted a place beside her for Matt to sit down.

With a quick mocking grin at Liz, he settled down beside her daughter.

'So what do you do? And how do you know my mum?'

21

CHAPTER TWENTY ONE

Andrew was drunk. Way beyond drunk. He was seriously pissed. He staggered out of the pub, his foot caught on the step, and he would have fallen if Kevin hadn't grabbed him. 'Thanks mate,' he slurred.

A couple of young girls walked past. He leered and winked. They laughed at him and kept walking. 'Slags,' he called after them.

Kevin took his arm and led him in the opposite direction. 'How's your girl?' Kevin asked.

Andrew frowned at the thought of her. 'Useless bitch, just like her mother was.'

'Not seen her for a while' Kevin said casually, 'she must be what? Twelve?'

'Nearly fourteen,' Andrew said before dropping to the curb to throw up.

Kevin smiled to himself. 'Is she now? Doesn't time fly?'

Andrew staggered to his feet. Kevin took his arm. 'Come on mate, let's get you home.'

. . .

Chapter 21

KYLIE HEARD them stumbling down the drive. She heard voices and the key in the door. She strained to listen; if he had a woman with him, then she'd be left alone. She heard a man's voice, and it wasn't her father's. She pulled the covers high up around her as tears fell silently down her cheeks. The front door closed, and she heard the kitchen door open. The mutt gave one brief bark; she heard her Dad as he fussed the stupid animal, and she heard the footsteps on the stairs. Only one set, but they were heavy. The floorboards creaked and groaned and she knew the man was heading her way.

She glanced at the door. The feeble barrier of the drawers wouldn't save her. She started to shake. Her eyes darting around looking for escape, but she knew there wasn't one. Not for her. The door handle turned. Then pressure against the door, the drawers slid slowly towards the wall.

Kylie buried herself under the covers and closed her eyes. If she shut them tight enough and wished hard enough, she might get lucky and die.

KEVIN PAID the taxi and climbed out. He walked to his front door a contented man. Sometimes life was good. He let himself in and turned around to lock and bolt the door. He didn't share Andrew's view on the killer. Kevin had a bad feeling about it and wasn't taking any chances.

Without switching the hall light on, he went into the kitchen. He was famished. Sex always made him hungry, and she had been as sweet as honey. He pulled open the fridge door and the kitchen light flicked on. For a brief second, he didn't get it. Didn't register what was happening. Then, as realisation hit him, so did the fear. He swung round to face the black-clad figure who was pointing a gun at him.

On his kitchen table was a note. He stepped closer to the table and read it – ON YOUR KNEES AND WRITE **SORRY WITH THE LIPSTICK**. Kevin picked up the lipstick. It was new and unused. His hand was shaking violently and he could feel beads of sweat bursting through his pores. He fought his fear. He had to remain calm and in control.

He looked at the figure, assessing. They had a gun; they knew how to use it, but the killer wasn't large, they were medium height, slim build. And despite the gun, Kevin felt he had an advantage – as he had nothing to lose.

Kevin dropped the note to the floor and looked at the figure defiantly. 'No.'

The killer stepped closer and pointed the gun at Kevin's head. Adrenaline pumped through Kevin's veins, making him brave and reckless. If the killer would come just a little closer, he could make a lunge for it. He stood resolute. 'You're going to kill me anyway, so just do it.' He was pleased with his bravado. He'd show the fucker what he was dealing with.

A shot rang out, and a bullet seared into his knee. He screamed in pain and dropped to the floor. 'Fuck! Alright! Alright...'

The figure moved around the table and kicked the lipstick closer to him. Kevin concentrated all his pain and fury into a sideways lunge and grabbed the killer's leg. The intruder toppled backwards and dropped the gun. Kevin launched himself at the killer, dragging his bleeding leg he threw himself on top and punched the figure hard in the ribs.

He grabbed the balaclava and pulled it from their head.

Chapter 21

He stared in stunned surprise. His face was close against theirs.

A knee shot up and caught him in the groin. He screamed in agony. The killer pushed him off and scrambled to their feet, then stamped on his shot leg. The pain sent him fighting for consciousness.

The killer lunged for the gun and turned it on him.

The question formed in his mind and reached his lips... 'Why?' But the bullet hit before he could compute any answer.

22

CHAPTER TWENTY TWO

I'd been careless. I should have been more careful. I knew how dangerous Kevin was. He had been the ringleader. The master manipulator. How had I let him get the better of me?

Time was against me now. There would be clues, stuff for forensics to get excited about. It wouldn't be long before they were knocking at my door. How long did I have? I wasn't sure, but it would take time to do the checks.

In all our research, we never considered being caught before we had finished. It seemed insanely arrogant now. But we had planned it all so carefully we didn't see how it could go wrong. But then we never considered me having to do all this alone either.

I was sure I still had time. They might suspect, but the evidence would have to be pieced together. It was a warning though; I had to speed up, and I had to smarten up. After twenty years of planning, I wasn't going to be stopped now.

. . .

Chapter 22

MATT DIDN'T WANT to wake up. But someone was banging on his door. Reluctantly, he opened his eyes. It was still dark, and he glanced at his bedside clock. It was just gone four am. He threw the covers off and climbed out of bed. He ran downstairs and pulled open the door. A young uniformed PC was on his doorstep.

His first thought was Avril. Had she done something stupid? Had they found her in a ditch, was she dead?

Matt didn't get to a second thought. 'They have sent me to get you.' The PC said. The lad seemed very young, hardly old enough to hold a driving license.

Or was it just that he was getting old? 'By?'

'DS Tyson sir, there's been another murder.'

Matt opened the door wider. 'You'd better come in while I throw some clothes on.' He didn't wait for an answer; he headed back upstairs to his bedroom.

He picked up his mobile, which listed several missed calls. The empty bottle of whisky by the bed told him why he hadn't heard them.

MATT KNEW who was dead as soon as they turned into the street. It was where Kevin lived; it was a neat and tidy, semi-detached pre-war house. Matt knew Kevin had lived there his entire life, man and boy. Matt had even gone there once as a lad. Kevin's mother had invited a few 'friends' home for tea after school. He never understood why he'd been asked or even why he went. He and Kevin had never been friends. But it had been Kevin who issued the invitation, and even back then when they were barely teenagers, you didn't say no to Kevin. Not unless you were up for a kicking.

Not that Matt had been a coward. But Kevin had a way of getting what he wanted. He was a clever manipulator. He

CHAPTER TWENTY TWO

was brilliant at assessing others' weaknesses, and then he'd exploit them ruthlessly.

Somehow Kevin had made Matt feel that by turning down the invitation it would hurt Kevin's mother's feelings. Utter nonsense, of course, since she'd never even met him. But Matt had gone along to the 'Tea' party. He hadn't liked Kevin's mother at all. She'd been everything a perfect mum should be. Lots of homemade cakes and sandwiches, they even got Coca-Cola, a real treat that he rarely experienced at home. The woman had been attentively asking all the boys about school and about her son and about the teachers and the girls.

To start with, it had been flattering. Matt's own mother worked part time, and he had two younger brothers, so he wasn't used to a lot of adult attention. But then it had felt invasive. More like an inquisition. None of the other lads had seemed bothered or fazed by it. But Matt couldn't wait to get away and he made sure that he never went back again. It had felt as though he was in a play and everyone else knew the plot and what their lines were; he was the only one who didn't get it. Kevin and his mother had some other agenda and Matt had been too stupid or to naive to know what it was.

Jen walked out of the house as soon as she saw him arrive. She was excited. 'This one fought back,' she said the minute he climbed out of the car. 'He was shot in the leg and the head. He didn't write sorry, although the lipstick is there...'

Matt quashed the irritation he usually felt at seeing Jen all bright and bouncy at such a shit hour. Truth was she could keep him out of the loop and take over. Since his wife was a suspect, he should really be off the case. But they had no evidence, and she hadn't been charged with anything.

Besides, he was an experienced officer, and the force was overstretched and short staffed. He walked into the house. Kevin was a bloody heap on the kitchen floor. Matt knew he should feel some sadness and compassion. The man was dead, had probably died in agony. But he didn't, and if he was brutally honest with himself, he was glad.

A uniformed PC waved at Matt to get his attention. Matt left the kitchen and followed the police officer to a small room at the back of the house. It was a small study, dominated by an enormous desk and an expensive-looking computer. It also had a small comfy looking sofa, a very large TV and a DVD player. The police officer pointed to a fancy-looking printer, which was on the desk alongside a digital camera.

Matt had a horrible feeling that was quickly confirmed when the police officer pointed to the printer tray.

'Some pretty hard core shit. Children Sir…'

Matt stared at the pictures and shook his head in disgust. He wished he'd put a bullet in the bastard himself.

MATT SAT at the bar in the Rugby clubhouse, a pint in his hand and a photo in front of him. It was the picture of the team when they won the youth trophy.

Andrew walked in he stopped beside Matt and ordered himself a pint. He pointed to the picture. 'Not you an' all. Kev was whittling on about the past last night.'

Matt stared at the photo, wishing as he had a hundred times before that he could turn the clock back and relive that day.

'That was a real team.' Andrew said. 'Don't make 'em like that now. Kids today don't have the heart or the guts for it.'

'You were with Kevin all evening?'

CHAPTER TWENTY TWO

Andrew nodded.

'Until what time?'

'I dunno. Got a bit pissed, to be honest. We went back to mine, think I must have had more than I realised 'cause I woke up this morning on the sofa with Brucie slobbering all over me...'

'What about Kevin?'

'Went home, I guess. What the fuck is this about?'

'Anyone at home with you?'

'Kylie was upstairs.'

Matt finished his drink and stood up. He picked the photo up and folded it carefully in half before putting it into his pocket. Then he looked at Andrew. 'Change your lock.' He said seriously.

Andrew was surprised. He shook his head. 'You're just being paranoid...'

Matt stared at the other man, watching closely for a reaction. 'Kevin's dead. Shot early this morning.'

Andrew looked shocked, really shocked, and more than a little bit scared. Matt walked away.

23

CHAPTER TWENTY THREE

He was sick of the looks. Some were pitying, some were mocking, some were curious, and a couple were malicious. He wanted to get out and stay out, but he wouldn't give any of them the satisfaction. He sipped his coffee and kept himself shut away at his desk. The office was small and luckily it had been pretty empty for most of the day. He had a list of names and phone numbers in front of him and was ringing his way down the list. It was every name from the photo he took from the Rugby club. Most he remembered and the few that he didn't he got from the newspaper archives. At the time of the win, they had judged it to be newsworthy enough to warrant a full name list of the winning players, along with a copy of the photo. There they were in grimy black and white print, the victorious team.

Two players had already died, one from cancer and one in a road accident. Two had moved out of the area and he was struggling to find them. One had emigrated to Australia, Four were dead, shot by the killer and the rest he was trying

CHAPTER TWENTY THREE

to contact to tell them to change their locks and be extra careful. It was proving to be very difficult.

He looked up as Jen came hurrying into the office. He casually covered up the list. She had that look of determination and contained excitement that he'd come to dread.

'Socos found a hair,' she said.

He knew there was more to come. He was right.

'A woman's hair,' she added, looking directly at him.

Matt knew from her expression what was coming.

'Long and dark,' she paused. 'Gov, we went to your house, Avril wasn't there. Do you know where we can find your wife?'

'No.'

'Gov…'

He shook his head. 'She left. I've no idea where she went. But I do know that you are wrong. Avril might be lots of things, but she isn't a killer.'

Jen looked at him, and he had a horrible feeling he saw pity in her eyes. 'DNA won't match,' he said adamantly.

'We just need to talk to her Gov, see where she was last night.'

Matt knew she was right. Obviously Avril needed to be eliminated as a suspect. He scribbled down a couple of addresses and handed the paper to Jen. 'Couple of her friends, she might be with them.'

Jen took it and they looked at each other awkwardly.

'So she wasn't at home with you last night then?'

He shook his head. 'No, told you she moved out…'

'I'm sorry,' Jen said with what looked suspiciously like pity in her eyes.

She left and Matt felt a pang of guilt. Avril wouldn't appreciate the police turning up at her friend's house. But then, if she had nothing to hide… he let the thought trail away. There was a small nagging doubt, which seemed to be growing bigger in his head. He questioned how well he really knew her. She had always kept him apart from her family and rarely spoke about them. Hell, they hadn't even attended the wedding. He hadn't considered it strange. He knew some families just didn't get on and besides; they got hitched on a beach in Florida. His parents and their new spouses attended along with some of their mutual friends, but she had no family with her at all. In hindsight, he should have asked more questions, been more curious, but his energies were diverted by trying to keep his sniping parents apart. Hindsight was a wonderful thing! Don't they say that everyone has a secret? Although he never knew who 'they' were. What if Avril's was so huge and so dark that it had turned her into a vengeful killer? Plus, there was still the question of where was she between leaving Brian's house at twelve and turning up at home, just a ten-minute drive away, nearly two hours later.

He stood up from his desk and stretched. While Jen was tracking Avril down, he decided to do a bit of digging of his own.

ANDREW WAS SOBER, and worried by the news that Kevin was dead. The pub was on the edge of town and not a place he usually visited. Certainly not a place you'd take a girl on a date. It was a dump, a dangerous dump.

Two men looked up when he entered. One of the men made a small movement with his head, enough to let Andrew know that he was in the right place. Both men were smoking. Above them, on a wall was a no smoking sign. Someone had written 'fuck you' across it.

Andrew sat down opposite the men and pulled an envelope from his pocket. He glanced around nervously, but no one was paying any attention to them or their transaction. He passed the envelope to one of the men.

The man peeled it open and glanced inside. His fingers ran across the top of the wad of notes, seemingly to check the amount. Although it was far too fast an assessment for him to have counted it. Apparently satisfied, he handed a package to Andrew. It was small but bulky and wrapped in a thick paper bag. The type that shops used now instead of plastic ones, a save the earth type bag. Andrew took it and thought it might just be a save the Andrew bag. He smiled at his own joke and with a brief nod to the men, the silent transaction was complete.

Andrew drove himself home. The package was on the seat beside him. He knew he should keep it hidden and out of view, but he liked to know it was within easy reach. He liked the fact that he had it and wondered why he'd never thought to get one before. Trust Kevin to have contacts like that. He didn't want to think about Kevin. Couldn't believe he was really dead. He turned the radio up and blanked it from his mind.

He knew he'd have to find a hiding place at home. The local paper had reported that Edward had been shot in his bedroom, so maybe that was the place to stash it.

KYLIE HEARD the car pull up onto the drive. That was unusual. It was early evening. He never came home till late, and rarely by car. He was normally too pissed to drive. She got up from her desk where she'd been on her laptop and went to the window. She saw him climb out of the car and lock it. He had something in his hand; he was hugging it tight against him as if to shield it or hide it away.

Chapter 23

She heard the front door open and then steps on the stairs. He didn't go to the kitchen first to see the mutt, that wasn't normal. She hadn't pushed the drawers in front of her door; she hadn't expected him home for hours. No time to do it now. Not that it would save her, anyway. Not from him or his bastard friend.

She heard him on the stairs; he hadn't checked on Bruce first. The dog was barking loudly, but her father carried on up to the landing. The footsteps hurried straight past her room; he didn't even pause. Something was wrong. She didn't want to leave her room, although it was hardly a sanctuary. She was just as vulnerable there as anywhere else. But it just felt safer.

But she knew she had to know what was going on. Kylie pulled her door open slowly, carefully, hoping it wouldn't creak. If it did, then she would just hurry straight to the bathroom. Even he couldn't punish her for having a pee.

It didn't make a noise. Barely daring to breathe, she crept along the landing. His door was open, Just a crack, but enough for her to see him on his knees in his room. Whatever it was he had brought from the car was now being shoved under the mattress.

Maybe it was money. If he had a cash stash, then it might be enough for her to run away. She'd have to act fast though, because he never kept money for long. That's why mum had left. He'd drank or gambled his way through every penny he earned.

For the first time in months, possibly even years, Kylie felt the unfamiliar stirrings of hope and optimism. She could be free of him. And soon.

. . .

CHAPTER TWENTY THREE

MATT WAS ANNOYED. He had tracked down Avril's grandmother. He had met the lady once, just before they got married. He remembered her as old and frail even then, amazingly she was still alive. The care worker at the nursing home told him that Mabel had just celebrated her ninetieth birthday.

'She gets a little bit confused…' the care worker said.

That was an understatement. Mabel had skin as thin as parchment that was as brown and wrinkly as a walnut. But her eyes were bright and alert and she seemed lively and happy.

'Hello Mabel,' he said gently, 'Do you remember me? I'm Avril's husband?'

'Of course I remember you,' she said beaming from ear to ear showing off remarkably good teeth for someone so old.

Encouraged, he sat down opposite her. 'I need to ask you about Avril, about her parents.'

'Who dear?'

'Your granddaughter Avril.'

Mabel looked at him blankly for a minute then she started to hum a tune, something catchy and vaguely familiar. He had a feeling he was losing this one. He tried again.

'Mabel…'

She stopped humming and smiled at him, that bright white toothy grin again. Either she had the country's best dentist or they were false.

'Hello.' She said, looking at him with a questioning gaze as though he had just arrived.

'Mabel, I need your help, Avril needs your help.'

'I have a granddaughter called Avril.'

Matt nodded.

'I have a granddaughter called Avril,' she repeated.

Chapter 23

'Yes, you do. Are her parents still alive?'
'Of course they are.' She said looking annoyed and lucid.
'So why doesn't Avril speak to them?'
'Because of Ted.'
'Who's Ted?'

Mabel's gaze slid away from him, and she started to hum again.

MATT WALKED down the high street. He entered the gym, but he hadn't really gone for a workout. He'd hoped to see Liz. But she wasn't there, and he didn't think another impromptu visit would be welcomed by her. So he was heading home to an empty bed and an empty life.

He managed to avoid the pub. But he found himself standing at the checkout of the twenty-four-hour convenience store with a bottle of whisky in his hand.

He glanced out of the window and was surprised to see Jen. She was dressed to impress. Her hair was loose and her face was made up. The trousers had disappeared, and she had legs; she was wearing a short skirt and high heels; she scrubbed up well. He put the bottle down and moved closer to the window. She wasn't alone; she was with a man. A tall young man, they were walking arm in arm and the man bent down to kiss her. Matt stood transfixed. Was she really that stupid? Or maybe she didn't know? She hadn't been in town for long; it was possible that she really didn't know who he was? Either way, it gave Matt a certain satisfaction; it seemed she wasn't so perfect after all. He pulled out his mobile phone and took a quick picture; it might have some tease value to it if she got too pushy or too cocky.

. . .

CHAPTER TWENTY THREE

Liz was restless, drifting in and out of sleep as she fought the dreams that wanted to drag her back to the past.

A young Liz and her sister Melissa were close to the DJ. The pub was crowded and smoky; a small area had been cleared of tables and chairs and was being used as a dance floor. The DJ put another record on and then turned his attention to Melissa. He pulled her into his arms and kissed her. Liz was grinning happily. She had a glass in her hand and was leaning against the wall.

The DJ, Steve, glanced over at Liz. He looked down at Melissa, 'she alright?'

Melissa turned her head just in time to see her sister slide down the wall. Melissa and Steve rushed over. Liz was sitting on the floor, a silly grin on her face.

'She's pissed.' Steve said, amused.

Melissa took the glass from Liz, which was miraculously still upright and clasped in her hand. She sniffed it and then tasted it. Melissa looked at Steve. 'She was supposed to be drinking Cinzano, this is gin...'

Steve helped Liz to her feet.

'You should marry my sister. She's in love with you,' Liz said in a slow, slurred voice.

Steve glanced across at a blushing Melissa. 'Is she now?'

'Yep, she told me so.'

'Liz!'

Melissa took her sister from Steve, who was looking very pleased with himself. The record was reaching its end, and he had to change it.

'Better get her outside,' He said. 'Fresh air will help to sober her up. There's a seat at the bus shelter just around the corner. I finish in half an hour. I'll take you both home then.'

Chapter 23

Melissa nodded her head and started to walk away, supporting her sister.

Steve called after her. 'Mel...'

She turned her head. 'Yes?'

He grinned. 'I love you too.'

LIZ OPENED her eyes and waited for the dream to fade. She climbed out of bed and headed for the shower.

Dried and dressed, Liz made herself a coffee. The toast popped up, and she smothered it with butter. Sam was at the kitchen table still in her pyjamas, tucking into a bowl of cereal.

Both women looked up as the kitchen door opened, and Craig entered the room. He was fully dressed in his biking leathers and looked ready to hit the road. 'Thanks for having me, Lizzie.'

Liz was surprised. 'You're off? Now?'

Craig glanced at Sam, but she concentrated on her cereal.

'Yeah, got to, lessons, you know...'

He leant down to kiss and hug Sam, who stopped munching long enough to return his affections.

Liz waited until Craig had left, then she stared hard at her daughter, who eventually had to give in and look at her mother.

'What?'

'Are you going to tell me? Or do I have to run after Craig and beat the truth from him?'

Sam smiled at the idea of her mother taking on her six foot plus boyfriend. 'I've been told to take some time off.'

'You're sick?'

'Kinda. Bad dreams and panic attacks.'

CHAPTER TWENTY THREE

Liz sank down into the chair beside Sam and took her hand. 'Oh love, for how long? I don't understand. You seemed fine when you went off to Uni. Are you eating properly? Sugars stable?'

Sam nodded her head and pointed to her little black pouch on the table. It held all her testing strips and blood sugar reader along with her insulin pen.

Sam looked healthy enough. She was a good colour and had been bright and cheerful the last few days. Liz was upset. She'd really thought her daughter had gone off to University strong and confident and ready to take on the challenge.

'Of course I am. It was fine,' Sam said. 'At least to start with. The doc said it's very common when you leave home for the first time.'

'I suppose so. A bit scary, new environment and new friends...'

Sam looked at her mother in surprise. 'It's not about me mum. I really am fine.'

Liz was confused. 'Then what?' suddenly she realised. 'Not me? Oh love, please tell me you haven't made yourself ill worrying about me.'

Sam began to cry. Liz pulled her daughter into her arms and fought back her own tears.

'Oh mum, I just have this feeling that something terrible is going to happen.'

'Oh, love...'all she could do was hold her daughter tight.

MATT KNEW he could leave Jen to do the briefing. That no one would really expect him to do it. The incident room had been dismantled and reassembled in a much larger room.

Chapter 23

More staff had been drafted in and another board had been added with Kevin's details.

Matt stepped into the front of the room, 'it seems we have a serial killer on our patch.' Good one mate, he thought to himself, start by stating the bleeding obvious! He took a deep breath and carried on. 'Good news is we might have a bit more luck evidence wise with this one.'

Jen stepped forward. 'We're waiting on results but he had a hair in his hand, several actually, although as yet we don't know if there was a follicle to get enough DNA from. They were long and dark...' she paused to glance at Matt. 'It's possible they belong to a woman. We need to know where he was and what he was doing early that evening. We need to trace and eliminate everyone who he had any contact with.'

'Do we have any suspects?'

Everyone turned and looked at the young DC who had been drafted in from a nearby station.

Jen cleared her throat. There were a few sniggers, and the lad looked around him in confusion. Matt wondered if one of his team had told him to ask the question.

Matt looked directly at the detective constable. 'We have a woman helping us with our enquiries,' he said.

Jen nodded her head.

'You should also be aware that he was into child pornography,' Matt said, fighting the surge of anger that struck him whenever he thought about what he'd seen at Kevin's house. 'His computer is being searched and analysed. We need to follow every lead that this throws up. Is it possible that they were all part of a paedophile group? This might be a vigilante killing...'

Was it possible? Could it be all about porn? Could he really be let off the hook that easily?

'We also need to establish how it is that the killer just walks into every house. We know that two of the victims had new front doors in the last five years, and we need to check on the installation companies.' Jen said.

Matt looked around the room and then at Jen. 'One more thing. The press is clamouring for details. Even the nationals have picked it up now. I'm sure I don't need to remind any of you that talking to them about this case is not permissible.'

Jen nodded her head in agreement, and Matt smiled to himself. So she really doesn't know then.

Everyone left the room apart from Matt and Jen.

'Did you find her?' He asked, lowering his voice.

'Yes.,' she replied. 'I spoke to her yesterday. Her alibi is a bit iffy; she stayed in and went to bed early. Her friend confirmed it, but she could easily have slipped out later that night. She has agreed to give a DNA sample; she's coming in this morning.'

Matt looked for Liz, but she didn't seem to be in the station. He wanted to check the rota and see when she was working, but that felt a bit stalkerish. So instead he went to his desk and carried on trying to contact the people on his list to warn them to change their locks. Given the new twist in the case with the paedophile angle, he didn't feel the same worry or urgency now. But it gave him something to do and took his mind off how much he wanted to see Liz.

He saw Avril arrive; he had been looking out for her. They walked into the corridor and greeted each other awkwardly. Aware of the spying eyes of his colleagues, he steered her round the corner, beyond the view of his office. He would have liked to take her into one of the interview rooms, but he didn't feel that would be appropriate. It might raise eyebrows and questions, since she was still a suspect.

Chapter 23

'Who is Ted?' he asked her, deciding that the direct approach was the only one to take.

Her face flushed an angry red. 'Who told you about him?' she snapped with more fury than he'd ever seen in her.

Jen walked around the corner and stared at them uncertainly.

Avril stabbed Matt in the chest with her perfectly manicured fingernail. 'Stay out of my life.' Then she turned her back on him and hurried towards Jen.

All Matt could do was stare after her, shocked and more than a little worried.

24

CHAPTER TWENTY FOUR

Matt looked around the gym and was disappointed to find that Liz wasn't there. He had no idea how she had got under his skin so quickly or easily. There was something about her that had grabbed him from the moment he first saw her, and since then thoughts of her had dominated far too much of his time.

His marriage was in tatters, so maybe that made him more susceptible to the charms of a beautiful lady, although he couldn't ever remember feeling like this when he first met Avril. They hung around in the same group and as couples paired off they somehow became a pair; it was almost by default rather than choice. They got on ok; laughing and joking and they seemed to be on a similar wavelength and did what all their friends were doing, they got engaged, twelve months later they were married, they bought a house and then they were supposed to have kids. That's when it all started to to go wrong. Until then they had both been on the relationship treadmill, jogging along, fulfilling everyone else's expectations. It was when the

Chapter 24

required baby failed to materialise that they both began to question why they were together.

Matt climbed onto the exercise bike and started at a slow to warm up pace. He gradually built up some speed and increased the gradient. He was soon sweating and struggling, and making his usual mental promise to quit smoking and get fitter. In the mirror, he saw Liz's daughter Sam enter the gym. Her eyes rested on him and she weaved her way through the machines towards him.

'I'm looking for mum,' she said with a big smile. She was tall and slim like her mum, but the similarity ended there. While Liz had dark hair and blue eyes, her daughter's hair was dark blonde and her eyes were what he thought would be described as hazel.

He slowed down, 'I haven't seen her this evening.'

'I was hoping she'd grab a bite with me. She's not at home, or answering her phone.'

Matt wiped his brow and climbed off the bike. 'Everything alright?' he asked, looking closely at her. She'd gone a little pale and her hands were trembling.

'I skipped lunch, I'm starving.' She did a small smile, but it wasn't very convincing, 'I need to eat...' she grabbed hold of the bike saddle and with the other hand she pulled her handbag towards her, but before she could open the zip she keeled over and dropped to the floor.

Matt went down on his knees beside her. He checked her pulse and placed her into the recovery position. A small crowd was gathering.

'She's out cold,' he said to the young staff member who had rushed to his side. 'Call an ambulance.'

'What happened?' Someone behind him asked.

He looked down at her and ran through the few seconds before she collapsed and remembered her going for her handbag. He reached across and picked it up from beside her. Opening it up and tipping it upside down; the contents spilling across the floor. He riffled through the usual selection, tissues, make-up bag, Tampax, small hair brush, purse, a couple of packets of mints, a small can of full sugar coke, a cola and a small honey pot.

'Should you be doing that?' A young woman asked. 'That's private stuff.'

He ignored her and picked up the mints and can of coke. He turned to the woman; she was young, slim and attractive. 'Do you or any of your friends have these in your handbag?'

She shook her head. 'Are you kidding? Those things are full of sugar.'

'Exactly,' he said more to himself. He grabbed the honey pot and opened it, it was small, the type you get in a hotel. Scooping a large blob onto his finger, he stuck it into Sam's mouth. He rubbed the honey around her gums and then repeated the process.

He could hear the sound of a distant siren. He tried the honey for a third time, but she was still out cold. Picking up the coke he opened it and touched her gently, 'Sam?' he called, but she was unresponsive.

The paramedics hurried towards them and Matt stepped aside to let them take over.

Liz was sitting on a hard chair in an empty corridor. Matt walked towards her carrying two take out cups. She glanced up at him as he approached; he sat beside her and handed her one of the cups. 'White with sugar.'

She opened her mouth to speak, but he cut in before she could.

'I know, I don't either. But you've had a shock so you

Chapter 24

need sugar, plus vending machine coffee tastes like shit, so it needs all the help it can get.'

Liz sipped the coffee and pulled a face that confirmed his own view.

'Any news?' he said gently.

'They're doing more tests, they want to keep an eye on her for an hour or two, and then hopefully she can come home. She'll be fine, this time...'

Matt took her hand. 'She's strong...'

'And sometimes stupid. She can't skip meals, she knows she can't. How many times does she have to be told?'

'We all break the rules sometimes,' he said.

Liz twisted in her chair to look at him. 'They told me what you did, with the honey. The paramedics said it could have been much worse, she could have gone into a coma...' she was struggling to hold back the tears. 'How did you know?'

'What teenager carries cola that isn't diet and a pot of honey around with them unless they are diabetic? Besides, my mum was the same, a type one diabetic. She was sometimes just too busy to stop and eat properly, she wouldn't realise her sugar levels had dropped and she had a problem until it was too late and she was keeling over. I think I knew how to open a jar of jam and stick a spoonful in her mouth even before I could walk!

Liz was tired, it had been a long and frightening night, even when they got back from the hospital she hadn't really slept. She dragged herself out of bed and into the bathroom. Twenty minutes later, showered and dressed, she stood in the doorway of Sam's bedroom staring at her sleeping daughter.

CHAPTER TWENTY FOUR

'Quit looking at me,' a sleepy voice muttered from under the duvet.

Liz walked further into the room. Sam was half awake, her eyes barely open. 'How are you feeling?'

'Much better,' Sam replied, looking sheepishly up at her mum.

'I can phone in sick, stay at home with you...?'

Sam pushed the duvet down from her face and twisted round to face her mother. 'Stop fussing mum,' she said,' go to work, I'll be fine, it was a stupid mistake. I promise I'll be more careful.'

Liz hesitated, still worried and not at all convinced about going to work.

'Honestly mum, my sugars are back under control. Go...' she shooed with her hands.

'Ok, but you promise to ring me if you feel even a tiny bit off. And make sure you eat properly.'

'Mum!'

'Ok, I'm going.' Liz turned and walked to the door.

'Oh, and mum...'

She turned and looked at her daughter.

'Thanks.'

Liz smiled, 'not really me that needs thanking,' she said.

25

CHAPTER TWENTY FIVE

Liz pulled up on her drive and climbed out of her car. The sun was shining, and it was a lovely spring evening. The young girl from next door waved as she hurried past. Liz smiled and waved back, and then she went indoors.

She put her briefcase down and hung her jacket up on the hook in the hall. She sniffed the air. 'Sam?' she called, before following her nose into the kitchen.

The room was chaotic, the aftermath of a baking explosion. Sam was busy at the hob. 'Go and get showered and changed,' she said shooing her mother out of the room.

'What's going on?'

'Surprise. Go...'

One of Liz's best dresses was laid out on her bed. Liz was surprised and pleased. If Sam wanted them to have a special evening, then she was more than willing. She had a quick shower and re-did her makeup. The dress was lovely. She remembered when she brought it. She had been with Dawn, whose birthday it was, they'd gone into London for a day of shopping followed by a trip to the theatre. It was expensive

CHAPTER TWENTY FIVE

and seemed extravagant, but Dawn had convinced her to buy the dress. It was soft red silk and fitted her perfectly. She'd only worn it once before. Her social life had little need for silk dresses.

As she walked down the stairs, she hoped that after a lovely evening she could persuade Sam to go back to University. Sam had always been sensitive. She should have realised that her own troubled and grieving mind wouldn't stay hidden from her daughter.

The kitchen chaos had been transformed. It was now clean and tidy. Something smelt amazing, and the table was laid with wine glasses and even a lit candle.

'Oh, Sam, it's lovely,' Liz said, looking around her in amazement. She did a twirl to show off the dress. Sam walked across the kitchen and hugged her.

'What's the occasion?' Liz asked.

The doorbell rang. 'Is Craig coming?'

Sam didn't answer; she hurried off to the front door. Liz took the chance to peep in the pans that were simmering on the hob. She turned around, smiling. But the smile froze when Matt followed Sam into the kitchen.

He was carrying a large bunch of roses and a box of chocolates.

'What are you doing here?' she demanded.

Matt turned to Sam, he looked confused. 'Um, I was invited?'

Sam grinned guiltily. 'It's all ready, so sit down.'

Matt handed the gifts to Liz, who was still trying to decide how to react. She looked at the chocolates and flowers. Matt shrugged his shoulders. 'Yeah, I know more clichés.'

Sam took the flowers from her mum and smelt them. 'Lovely. I'll put these in water. Mum loves roses.'

Chapter 25

Matt and Liz sat down. Liz looked at Sam. 'The table is set for two.'

Sam put plates onto the mats in front of them, followed by serving dishes. 'I ate while I was cooking. Besides, I've got work to do.'

'Sam.'

'Really mum, I can't afford to get behind...'

'This looks and smells amazing,' Matt said, helping himself to a warm bread roll.

'Yes, it does,' Liz agreed, watching her daughter as she hurried out of the kitchen. Sam suddenly stopped and went to the fridge. 'Almost forgot the wine.' She opened it and crossed back to the table, pouring it into the two glasses.

Liz picked up her glass and took a sip.

'Oh mum, where's the key for your study?'

Liz almost spilled her drink. A drop splashed onto her dress. Matt was watching her as she mopped it up.

'My laptop is playing up, I wanted to use your computer, but the door's locked and I couldn't find the key.'

Liz took a deep breath. She talked calmly and even managed to smile. 'I can't seem to find it myself. Use my laptop; it's in my briefcase in the hall.'

Sam left happy enough. Liz looked at Matt. 'Let's eat,' she said, knowing that she should kick him out of house and never let him back through the door again.

KYLIE WAS in her father's bedroom. She was on her knees unwrapping the package that he had hidden under the mattress.

It was a handgun.

She dropped it in shock and surprise.

She heard a car pull up outside. The engine stopped, the

door shut, then footsteps approaching the house. Her father was home. She panicked. The key was already in the door. Hopefully, he'd go to the dog first. She quickly wrapped the gun up again as she heard the front door open. She pushed it back into position under the mattress. Footsteps on the stairs. He was coming; she checked the room was the same as when she entered and then ran out of the door and rushed straight for the bathroom and quickly pulled open the door just as her father reached the top of the stairs. She escaped into the loo and quickly locked the door behind her.

MATT leant across and re-filled Liz's glass.

She looked at his still full, untouched one. 'Not drinking?'

'Driving,' he said, not wanting to elaborate on his complicated relationship with alcohol. She let it go. He was relieved.

'So why doesn't she understand you?'

Then not so relieved. He'd rather do the drink question than talk about Avril, especially given the slightly sarcastic tone used by Liz. 'Complicated,' he said.

'Life always is,' she finished her glass and re-filled it again herself.

'She wanted a baby,' he blurted out. Then, unable to stare at it any longer, he picked his glass up and drank the wine.

'And you didn't,' she said, handing him the bottle.

He felt ill at ease and more than a little embarrassed. He drank the second glass. 'Well, I do. Or at least I did. But it seems we can't, or at least I can't. Although tests suggest no reason why I can't...' he was babbling. And he had been so determined to prove to her what a great cool guy he was. Stop talking, he told himself.

'I'm sorry,' she said.

'Don't be, probably for the best. Our marriage was only ever tolerable, recently just awful. Not fair to bring a child into that,' he filled both glasses again and drank his straight down.

'Maybe not. Is there nothing you can do?'

Matt shook his head 'She moved out,' he paused, took a deep breath, and then blurted out the rest. 'She was having an affair.'

'I'm sorry.'

'I'm not. It's a relief, for both of us. Truth is, I'm not good at this relationship stuff. I work stupid hours and I probably drink too much...' he paused and looked across the table at her. 'And I have no idea why I'm telling you all of this.'

Why was he telling her all of this? He had to stop drinking. Any minute now she'd start feeling sorry for him. Was he determined to always be a looser?

'So why are you such a tormented soul?' She said.

'Is that what I am? Tormented?'

He reached across the table and took her hand. She didn't pull away. Encouraged, he leaned over and kissed her.

They both jumped back as the kitchen door opened and Sam breezed in. She looked chuffed to bits at how close they were. 'Don't mind me. I'm exhausted, going to bed early.' She managed a yawn. 'I'll sleep like a log. I am really, really tired.' With a glass of water, she left the kitchen.

'My subtle daughter.'

Matt laughed. 'Well, she is really, really tired.'

He leant forward to kiss her again. Not gently this time, but urgently. Encouraged by her response, he stood up and moved around the table. He wrapped his arms around her waist and pulled her against him. She let out a small cry of pain and he released her immediately.

'I hurt you?'

'No. No, I slipped on the stairs, hurt my side. I'd forgotten it was there. Just a bruise.'

He moved closer again. Staring at her lips. 'You're sure?'

Liz put her arms around his neck and kissed him. He pulled her against him, but gently this time, careful to avoid her bruised side.

'Let me stay?' he whispered into her ear.

She drew back and looked searchingly into his eyes. He thought she was going to turn him down.

'Well, after all that wine you can hardly drive home, can you?'

'Were you trying to get me drunk, woman?'

'You know, where you're concerned, I have no idea what I'm doing.'

She took his hand and led him upstairs.

KYLIE WAS IN DARKNESS. The only illumination came from her computer. The house was silent, and the drawers were up against the door.

She stared intently at the monitor. A range of handguns were on the screen. She clicked on one and it enlarged to fill the entire window. It was the same as her father had hidden under his mattress. She clicked the mouse again and a list of its specifications came up. She moved the mouse and clicked onto - operating instructions.

LIZ WAS LAYING naked in his arms. Her head was resting on his shoulder and for the first time in her life she understood why people lived and died for love. She didn't know how to say what was in her heart. Dawn had tried to tell her. But she'd never listened, never understood. She had considered herself incapable of the love and passion that she thought belonged only to poetry and Mills and Boon novels.

He gently stroked her hair. He was as silent as she was. They both had a new reality to deal with. Liz knew it had unleashed a force within her and it threatened everything she believed in, everything that she had planned.

He spoke quietly into the darkness. 'Have you ever wished you could travel back in time? To relive one moment, one stupid misjudged moment, and take a different turn?'

Liz closed her eyes. 'Yes.'

He twisted around and lifted her chin. She opened her eyes. He looked searchingly into her face. 'Are forgiveness and redemption ever possible, or do sins always have to be accounted for? Can a tormented soul ever be saved?'

What could she say? In her heart she wanted to set him free, but her head said no. You can't re-write the past. And sins have to be paid for. She closed her eyes and turned away from him.

26

CHAPTER TWENTY SIX

Matt woke up and thought for one moment that he was dreaming, and then he remembered. She had her back to him; he moved close against her. He gently pushed her hair aside and started kissing the back of her neck. His hands were roaming. She stretched and relaxed back against him. 'I could get used to this,' he said, softly whispering.

Her hands clamped over his and removed them from her body. She climbed out of bed, grabbed a robe and wrapped it around her before turning to face him.

'Liz?' Matt said in confusion.

'I've got to get ready for work,' she said hurrying for the bathroom.

Matt closed his eyes. He was hurt. What just happened?

He dressed and went down to the kitchen. He guessed Sam must have been up early as the table had been cleared and the dishwasher was on. Making himself a coffee, he sat down at the table to wait.

Sam walked in, smiled when she saw him and helped herself to a bowl of cereal before sitting down beside him.

Chapter 26

Then Liz entered the kitchen. She barely looked at either of them. She made herself busy at the sink, even though it was already clean.

Matt stood up. 'Thanks for a lovely meal, Sam...'

Sam nodded and smiled.

Matt stood behind Liz. 'See you then...'

'Yeah, bye,' she said without turning around.

Defeated and gutted, he left.

He was just about to get into his car when Sam called after him. She ran out of the house, still in her pyjamas.

'She doesn't mean it.'

'Mean what?' Matt said. It hurt too much for him to care.

'To push you away. She likes you, I know she does.'

Matt wanted to be convinced, but he could only take so many slaps.

'It's been tough for her, well for both of us, since the accident. She lost her husband.'

'Your Dad died?'

'Well, he wasn't actually my Dad,' Sam said. 'Although he was a bloody wonderful substitute. He was killed in a crash, almost two years ago.'

They looked at each other; Matt nodded his head in understanding and climbed into his car.

LIZ HEARD HIM DRIVE AWAY. She knew she had been harsh, but what choice did she have? She should never have allowed him into her life, and definitely not into her bed. Liz picked up her handbag and left the house.

Liz stood in the doorway of the dance studio and watched as Phillip swirled Dawn around the room in some incredibly sexy version of a South American dance. It finished with him staring down at Dawn, deep into her eyes.

Then abruptly he stood up, let her go, and turned off the music.

Dawn looked across and saw Liz. She walked across the dance floor, a worried frown on her pretty face. 'What are you doing here? Is everything alright?'

Phillip waved to them both and left the studio. Liz really felt for her friend, for the first time understanding her pain.

'That was amazing.'

Dawn gave an elegant shrug. 'See if the judges agree on Saturday.'

'Well, watching that Dawn, I'd have to say that he is totally in love with you.'

Hope lit up in Dawn's eyes. But only briefly. Reality soon took over. 'Yeah, he is when we're dancing. That's what makes us such an excellent team.'

'Surely not just with the dancing, I saw the look in his eyes.'

'Yeah, bone melting isn't it. Sure he cares. Sure, he trusts and respects me, and actually I think he does love me as a friend. But I want what you see on the dance floor. I want that love…'she laughed sadly. 'But I'm not going to get it. Sometimes I think he's afraid of the potential between us…'

Liz could relate to that feeling. It was strange and new and definitely frightening. She knew that love – as in that irrational passion that could render a sensible person senseless had no place in her life. Maybe Phillip felt the same. 'I'm sorry,' she said with feeling.

Dawn shrugged her shoulders, a resigned and slightly sad expression on her face, 'anyway what are you doing here? Shouldn't you be at work?'

'I should, but I have a few things that need to be done. You got half an hour?'

'Of course.'

Chapter 26

Liz led the way from the dancing studio to the modern shopping centre. Milltown was far more progressive and prosperous than Bidbury. She stopped at a door and Dawn looked up at the nameplate.

'Solicitors? Liz, what's going on?'

MATT PULLED into his parking space at the police station. He was late. He'd spent a long time under the shower at home, playing and replaying the previous night's events. How had it all gone wrong? Or was it just that it had all moved too quickly for Liz? That's what her daughter seemed to think.

He climbed out of the car. The national news teams had set up camp with their giant aerials on top of giant transmission rigs. Bidbury was certainly on the map now.

Jen was flushed and excited.

'Anything useful back from forensics yet?' he asked as soon as he entered the office.

'Expected later today,' she said waving a card at him. 'You saw them out there? The nationals! A reporter from the Sun gave me this...'

Matt stopped walking. 'You spoke to them?'

Jen quickly picked up on his tone and adopted an attitude of her own. 'Well, obviously not about the case.'

'No, you'd never be so unprofessional as to talk to the press.'

She frowned, but her spirits were too high to be dampened by him. He could almost see her calculating the odds for promotion with such a high-profile case. 'He gave me this though and made many suggestions about what he'd pay for a scoop.'

Matt took the card. 'I don't need to tell you what damage

CHAPTER TWENTY SIX

talking to...' he looked at the card... 'Del Carter would do to your career.'

'No Gov you don't. But I have some leads.' She sat down on one side of his desk and waited until he was sitting opposite her. Then she handed him a file. 'Two of the dead men used the same double glazing company and although one of them was five years ago, the company still has the name of the fitter who did the job. And guess what?'

'It was the same man.'

'Yep, but James hadn't had a new door or double glazing. But...' she looked at him excitedly.

Matt was tiring of her game, but he was trying to be patient. 'But?' he asked obligingly.

'His home was broken into about three years ago and a locksmith turned up the same day to fit a new lock...'

'Ok.'

'Well, the locksmith said the insurance company had sent him. Since James didn't have to pay, he was happy enough to go along with it. But...'

'Ok, enough with the buts. Just tell me.'

Jen looked like she was a five-year-old who had just been scolded. Matt was immediately sorry. 'Tell me,' he repeated in a more patient tone.

'James wife or ex as she is now, pointed out that they didn't have insurance, said they had nothing worth nicking.'

Matt absorbed the information. 'So why didn't they question it, or even tell the police?'

'Why would they? They got a free new lock. Only thing James was worried about was that the man might return for payment.'

'So do we know who this free fitter is?'

Jen smiled triumphantly. She held the ace.

'We do. James's wife asked for a card, and he actually

Chapter 26

gave her one. It's the same man that worked for the glazing company, doing a bit of freelancing.'

Jen pointed to the file on the desk. 'It's all in there.'

'An address?'

'Yep. It's a house in Milltown, about forty miles away.'

Matt picked up the file and stood up. 'I'll go see him.'

'Not much point Gov. He's dead.'

A nagging thought was growing, taking shape and form and scaring the hell out of him. 'I'll go anyway, talk to the neighbours, and see what I can find out.'

Jen waited until he was almost at the office door. Then she called him. 'Oh, and gov...'

He turned. 'Yes?'

'All the victims were members of the same youth rugby team.' She picked up a copy of the local newspaper and there it was on the front page. A picture of the winning team with the victim's heads circled in blood red.

Their eyes locked and held.

Matt walked out.

Liz walked Dawn back to the dance studio. 'Thanks for that,' she said.

Dawn looked serious and worried. 'Sure, anytime.'

'It's just a precaution. I need to know that if anything happens to me, she'll be alright.'

Dawn didn't look reassured.

'Just promise to always be there for her.'

Dawn nodded her head. She was fighting back tears. 'Liz? You're scaring me.'

'Just promise.'

'I promise. Of course I do.'

CHAPTER TWENTY SIX

Satisfied, Liz hugged her friend. 'And you'll do the other thing?'

Dawn nodded, curiosity and worry on her face.

Liz smiled with as much reassurance as she could fake, then she left forcing herself not to turn and look back.

She drove home deep in thought, thinking about what she had to do, and she stopped at the cemetery and walked across the damp grass to the gravestones. She looked down at them and spoke quietly. 'I'm so sorry Mel, I've let you down.' She turned to the grave beside her sisters. 'We worked so hard Steve to get it right, but I've failed. I've failed you both.'

A shadow fell across the stones. She spun around. It was her mother. 'What are you doing here?'

The elderly lady laid a bunch of flowers on Melissa's grave. 'She's my daughter.'

The anger inside Liz exploded. 'No! You put her there. You killed her.'

The old lady stood her ground. She looked sad and hurt, but it was clearly an old augment and an old accusation. 'Beth, you've got to let it go.'

'How can I let it go? She's dead; you made her feel dirty, guilty and ashamed.'

The old lady sighed. 'Yes, and I have to live with that. I have to forgive myself because that's the only way I can face each day.'

'Well, I don't forgive you.'

Liz's mother shook her head sadly. 'I know Beth, and that's your tragedy.'

The old lady walked away, every step an effort.

Liz sank down onto the grass and closed her eyes as the memories filled her head.

. . .

Chapter 26

STEVE HELPED the young Liz and Melissa into the front room. They were both in a terrible state. Emotionally numbed and physically battered. Cuts, bruises, dried blood, torn clothes.

'We've gotta call the police,' Steve said to their mother as she fussed over them with disinfectant and gauze.

'No.' their mother said.

Steve looked at her with disbelief. 'But they've both been raped.'

Their mother was dabbing at Liz's cuts with Dettol. 'Look at them,' she said as she carried on dabbing. 'What will it be like for them? Tests, questions and examinations, the men will say they asked for it, consented to it. It'll be their word against the men's. Who are the police going to believe?'

Steve was holding Melissa. But Melissa was sat stiff and unresponsive, just staring at nothing. 'They'll believe us.' Steve said.

'You were there? You saw it?'

'Well no, but...'

Mother shook her head. 'Two girls, dressed to show off what they've got, out late, drunk...'

Steve jumped up, he was furious. 'No! It's not like that. The bastards can't get away with it.'

Mother opened a tube of Savlon antiseptic cream and gently patted it onto Liz's cuts. It stung, but she was still too shocked to respond to any stimuli, even pain.

Steve grabbed the phone. 'I'm calling the police.'

Suddenly Melissa snapped out of her unresponsive state. 'No,' she said forcefully.

'But... Mel...'

'No,' she said again, emotionless and without looking at him. 'Mum's right.'

CHAPTER TWENTY SIX

Steve punched the door with frustrated fury. Melissa finally lifted her eyes to look at Steve and then at Liz.

Liz flinched when she saw the terrible burning pain and humiliation in her older sister's eyes.

'We tell no one,' Melissa said. She paused to make sure they were listening. 'Ever.'

LIZ PULLED a tissue from her bag, she wiped her eyes and blew her nose, and then she stood up. She looked down at the two gravestones. 'Goodbye.' She said before hurrying back to her car. She paused, key in hand. Her mother was clinging to the railing that circled the cemetery, looking as though she could hardly hold herself up.

Something shifted inside of Liz, a stirring of compassion. She took a few steps forward, then stopped as her anger and pain tried to resurface. Torn, she stood still while the internal battle played out. Then her mother stood up, took a clean lace hanky from her handbag, dabbed her eyes and blew her nose.

Liz remembered those hankies. Her mum always had a pile of them in her dressing-table drawer. They were bleached and ironed, carefully folded and smelt of lavender. As a child, she had one tucked under her pillow at night.

'Mum...' the sound escaped her lips, barely more than a whisper.

Her mother turned.

Liz didn't know how to take the step that could build a bridge between them, but her mother did and with age defying agility the lady closed the gap and pulled Liz into a tight sob soaked hug.

27
___

CHAPTER TWENTY SEVEN

'I didn't do it,' Avril said.

'I know,' Matt replied and realised he believed it.

'Am I in the clear now?'

She was looking at him with a mixture of hope, pain and panic. He wanted to reassure her, but he knew he had to be honest. 'Not quite. It's all circumstantial and there's not enough to charge you…'

'But I'm still a suspect?'

'Yes, I'm sorry.'

Avril shook her head. Matt had never seen his wife so scared. He wished he could offer her comfort, but those days were behind them. He looked around the room, 'this is nice,' he said lamely. She was staying at a friend's. He did not know which friend, and it certainly wasn't any of their mutual ones. He didn't want to ask, not about her friend, or about her job, or lack of it, or about how they had reached the point where awkward silence sat between them. But he knew there was something he had to ask her again. 'Who's Ted?'

She lifted her head and stared at him; he thought she

was going to refuse to answer, but then she started to cry. 'He was my baby,' she said.

It was Matt's turn to be surprised; he almost thought he had misheard.

'I got pregnant when I was just fourteen,' she said, silent tears running down her face, 'my parents made me have an abortion.'

'Shit. I'm so sorry...'

'I never forgave them. As soon as I was sixteen, I moved here to Bidbury to live with my Gran.' She placed her hand on her flat stomach. 'I called my unborn baby Teddy, but the truth is I never even knew if it was a boy or a girl.'

Matt stared at the woman he had married almost seven years ago and realised that he didn't know her at all. She had carried the secret through the years of friendship and dating, and on into marriage, with never a word, nor a hint. Was he blind and stupid, or was it simply that he had never cared enough to look beyond the surface of her perfect and poised facade? Or was the truth that protecting his own deep dark secret kept everyone outside his personal exclusion zone, including his wife.

He walked across the room, sat down beside her and took her into his arms, 'I'm so sorry,' he said, 'for everything.'

Matt left the house and walked slowly back to his car. Whatever lingering doubts he had about his wife's guilt evaporated. He had his own theory, an idea that had been forming in some corner of his brain, despite his best efforts to ignore it. It had to be faced, and it might as well be now. He climbed into his car and headed out of town.

. . .

Chapter 27

LIZ KNOCKED on Sam's door before she entered. Sam was lying on her bed, earphones in, listening to music. Liz watched her daughter for a few seconds until Sam opened her eyes and saw her standing there. Sam pulled the headphones out and sat up, smiling.

'I've got to go out tonight. Will you be ok?'

'Sure. Craig's coming over soon. Are you seeing Matt?'

Liz shook her head. 'No, I have to work.'

'Ok. But mum...'

'Yes.'

'He's alright, you know. I like him.'

Liz forced herself to smile. 'I know. I like him to.'

Liz started to close the door as she left. Then she stopped and looked at her beautiful daughter. One earphone was already back in Sam's ear.

'Sam...'

Sam looked up expectantly.

'I love you,' Liz said.

MATT WAS DESPERATELY TRYING to get into town. But life and particularly the traffic conspired against him. An accident had caused major delays, and he was getting nowhere fast. He tried ringing her phones. Her mobile and her house number, but she wasn't answering. Not to him, at any rate. He even tried Sam's mobile, but she wasn't answering either.

He thought about sending a squad car to pick her up from home, but that would compromise her and he didn't want to do that. His trip to Milltown had confirmed his suspicions, the sold house, a chat to the neighbours, and he had all the information he needed. Steve Bryant, her dead husband, was the lock fitter. He could guess the rest, he had his own memories from that night; it was easy to put it all

CHAPTER TWENTY SEVEN

together. But he could end it, cover it up. He'd already started to formulate a cover story. But he had to get to her first. He owed her, and whatever the price, he was willing to pay it.

Matt tried ringing numbers from his Rugby player list, it seemed the entire world was out and about and nobody answered their phones anymore. The car edged forward a few meters and then stopped again as traffic lights turned red. He tried Liz again. 'Come on, talk to me...' he pleaded. But she didn't. He threw his phone down in frustration and swung the car into an illegal U turn before turning into a side street. He'd have to take the back roads.

LIZ PUT her dark clothes on and shoved her balaclava and gun into her jacket pocket. She opened the large manuscript book that was on the desk and removed the keys from the back. Not all of them. She knew the ones she wanted. Then she locked the book away again and left the study. In the kitchen she put a note on the table for Sam, nothing long or emotional, it was just an address, a phone number and the words - Sam, this your Gran, look her up.

Outside, she walked confidently towards her car. It didn't matter if they saw her number plate. This would be the last outing, she knew that. It would take too long to use the push-bike she had used for the other hits. She needed to move fast to stand any chance of getting the job done.

The first hit was easy. Tim Taylor lived in a mobile home. He put up little resistance beyond begging for his life. When he'd finished writing on the grubby floor, he'd looked up at her and dared to ask why.

She shot him. A single bullet in the forehead and she hurried on her way. She wasn't sure if anyone had seen her.

Chapter 27

She thought she heard someone shout after her. But she didn't stop. There was no running or screaming behind her. She reached her car, climbed in and drove away.

He asked why?

HER SISTER HELPED the young Liz out of the pub. The sound of Kylie Minogue singing - I should be so lucky - followed them out. It was noisy outside. A large group of youths were singing and shouting as they made their way down the street.

Melissa helped her round the corner. A bus shelter was up ahead. It was a wooden one, like a little hut. Liz's head was spinning. She dropped to her knees. Melissa couldn't hold her up anymore.

'Come on, Lizzie,' her sister said, struggling to get her back on her feet.

One of the rowdy youths ran to help her. It was a much younger Andrew. 'Here, let me help you, sweetie.' He lifted Liz up easily and turned around to shout at the rest of the group. 'Come on, we have pretty wenches in distress.'

Melissa tried to regain control of the situation. 'We're fine, really. It's cool.'

But Andrew wasn't interested in anything she had to say. He had Liz in his arms and he liked it.

The rest of the pack was hurrying to catch up, Kevin and Brian leading them.

Melissa looked back towards the pub, wondering if she should run back and get Steve. But that meant leaving Liz alone with the youths.

Kevin put his arm across her shoulders and purposefully steered her towards the shelter, following Andrew and her sister.

CHAPTER TWENTY SEVEN

Andrew laid Liz down on one of the benches. Melissa tried to put herself between him and her sister, forcing herself to remain calm, but she couldn't quite hide the panic from her voice. 'Thanks. We'll be ok now. Dad'll be along in a minute to pick us up.'

Kevin and Andrew exchanged a look. Brian smiled, silent communication completed they moved closer.

Liz was sobering up. The menace of the moment was kicking into her consciousness. She sat up. The lads surrounding them had gone quiet. Like they knew something was about to kick off.

Kevin turned to the group. He scanned their faces – fear, panic, excitement. 'Give us some cover, we're gonna party.'

Liz managed to get to her feet and tried to run, but she didn't stand a chance against Andrew. He pulled her by her hair and yanked her back towards him.

Melissa screamed and ran to her aid. But she was captured by Kevin, who punched her in the face and threw her down onto the concrete floor.

Andrew was on top of Liz on the bench. She tried to scream, but he clamped his hand over her mouth. She bit him hard. He yelped with pain and hit her hard. 'You fucking bitch.'

One youth stepped forward as if to intervene. Brian floored him with a punch in the stomach. He smiled nastily at the lad on the floor. 'Lighten up...' he looked around the men, 'this is a party.' Silent agreement spread through the group. It wasn't easy to stand up against Brian, Andrew, and Kevin.

Melissa was face down on the filthy floor with Kevin pushing her head into the ground. She could hardly breathe, let alone scream as Kevin took her from behind.

Andrew leant down close to Liz's face. 'Scream and I'll

hurt her.' He paused to make sure that she understood. The terror in her eyes, all the confirmation he needed. Then he smiled, a horrible, sinister smile. 'Now be a good girl and we can all have some fun.'

Tears streamed down Liz's cheeks. But she didn't close her eyes. She looked defiantly into her attacker's face, imprinting him with hatred in her soul.

Kevin stood up and zipped his flies. He kept a foot on Melissa's back to keep her down. Sobbing into the dust, she tried to reach around and pull her skirt down to cover herself. But he kicked her hand away and pushed her skirt higher. Her face burned with pain, shame and humiliation.

Kevin looked around the group. 'Who's next?'

Kevin grinned victoriously and looked at the lad nearest to him. It was Adam. Nobody moved. Kevin grabbed him and shoved him towards Melissa. The lad tripped and fell down beside her. Melissa closed her eyes and turned her head away.

'Come on Adam, what are you? Man or virgin?' Kevin taunted.

The group of youths laughed nervously.

'You are...' he pointed at Adam, 'he is. He's a fucking virgin!'

Adam was on the floor being laughed at by his peers. He didn't like it. He did what they expected of him.

Kevin led the group as they chanted his name 'A-dam. A-dam...'

The sound hammered into Liz's brain as Andrew hammered into her. Hate, fury and anger blunted the pain. Finally finished, Andrew stood up and punched the air, like he'd just achieved something amazing. Kevin grabbed the next lad and thrust him forward to Andrew. Andrew smiled at the lad and pointed down at Liz. 'This one loves to party.'

CHAPTER TWENTY SEVEN

Liz was cold sober now and quickly calculated her options. She had none. Even if she did manage to get up and run for it, she couldn't leave her sister to endure this torment alone. A gang of fit young rugby players stood between her and the pub. She didn't stand a chance, she couldn't fight them and no one was close enough to hear her screams.

The lads were all enthused and excited. Kevin's taunts and chanting had worked them into a frenzy. Both the silence and the reticence had gone. Mob mentality had taken over.

Andrew leant down, his face inches from Liz. He grabbed her chin and turned her head to look at Melissa. Her sister was still and pale like a statue as the assault on her body continued. Andrew looked menacingly into her eyes. 'You won't be any trouble at all, will you, sweetie?'

LIZ SLOWED DOWN; tears were rolling down her face. She was driving way too fast and was afraid she would attract attention. A police car, siren on, sped past in the opposite direction; maybe someone did see her after all. It annoyed and upset her that the men who had attacked them seemed to have buried away their guilty pasts. It was as if they had erased that night from their minds. Surely they must have known the day of reckoning would come? Liz wiped her eyes with the back of her hand. She had a job to finish, and she had to concentrate.

MATT BANGED impatiently on her door. No answer. He hurried around the back of the house and tried the back door. Locked. He quickly removed his jacket and wrapped it around his hand, and smashed a window.

Inside, he headed straight for the study. Again it was locked. He gritted his teeth, squared his shoulders and ran at the door. It stayed solidly closed. He concentrated all his anger and frustration into his attack and launched himself at the wood again. This time the door creaked and groaned and splintered. Encouraged, he did it again and this time he smashed his way into the study.

He pulled open drawers and searched the contents. The largest one at the bottom needed a key for the lock on it. He pulled and pushed and in sheer frustration kicked at it. But it resisted his anger and held onto the secrets within.

Matt ran back downstairs and retrieved his jacket from the floor. He shook off the shards of glass and dug into his pocket for a penknife.

Back in the study, he set to work on the drawer again.

Liz parked the car and climbed out. It was an unassuming street. Terraced houses, each one tall and narrow like shoe boxes lined up in a row. It was still light and a few people were around. A little girl was skipping on her lawn and a man was washing his car. Liz walked casually along the street. Her balaclava was in her pocket. She fingered it impatiently. A woman called the little girl indoors for her tea. Liz kept on walking.

Looking in the wing mirror of a parked car, she saw the man pick up his bucket and go inside. Liz took her chance. She walked confidently, like she belonged, and headed down a drive to a front door. She pulled a key from her pocket and put it into the lock.

The key didn't turn. The door didn't open.

Shocked, Liz checked the key. It had a tiny label on with the letter C. C for Cane. Edward Cane. There was no mistake. She tried again. The door would not open. She looked at it. The door itself was several years old. She didn't need to look at it to know that her husband had fitted it. But the lock itself was shiny and new. She hesitated, unsure what to do next. Time was running out. Did she go straight on to the next one and let Cane escape with his life? No. He had to pay. She rang the doorbell.

Edward smiled at her uncertainly when he opened it and saw an attractive female on his doorstep. But the smile soon slipped when she shoved the gun into his stomach. Recognition etched on his face.

FINALLY, the lock on the drawer gave way to the pressure from Matt's pen knife. He found what he was looking for, but hoped he wouldn't find. Until that moment, he'd prayed that by some miracle he had it wrong. He lifted out a book and laid it on the desk.

He stared at it. THE BOOK OF REVENGE written in capital letters across the front.

Matt slumped down into the desk chair; all his nightmares had come alive. 'Oh Liz, what have you done?'

He touched it as though afraid it would burn his fingers, Matt opened up the manuscript book. It was full of clippings and a journal.

He started to read aloud, 'If you are reading this book, I assume I have finished my task and have handed myself in for punishment. I know what I have done is terrible. I'm not criminally insane, I know exactly what I've done and why. I hope this book will explain....'

Matt turned the page and continued to read. 'Our lives

Chapter 27

were normal, almost perfect until the night my sister and I were viciously and repeatedly raped....'

Matt didn't need to read on for the details of that night. They had remained locked away in his head, like a stalker hiding in the shadows. He'd spent twenty years running away from the memories. Now he had nowhere to run and nowhere to hide.

28

CHAPTER TWENTY EIGHT

A young Matt was singing and chanting along with the rest of the victorious Rugby team. Up ahead was the pub, Matt ran on and ducked inside to use the gents. As he entered the pub, two pretty girls were coming out. It was Melissa supporting a drunken Liz. He grinned at them and moved aside to let them pass.

When Matt came out of the toilets, the rest of the youths were out of view. He couldn't see them, but he could hear them. He followed the noise around the corner and caught up with them at the bus stop. Matt was very drunk, and he staggered a bit. He wasn't used to drinking.

Matt joined the crowd; he couldn't immediately comprehend what was happening. Kevin was taunting Adam; he seemed to want Adam to have sex with a girl who was face down on the floor. Andrew was with another girl on the bench. When Andrew finished, Kevin shoved James forward.

James was struggling to perform as the girls' eyes burned with hatred. 'Make her look away.' James pleaded.

Chapter 28

Andrew yanked her top up, exposing her breasts and covering her face.

Matt staggered forward, still slow to grasp the reality of what he was witnessing. He pointed to the girl on the floor. 'Is she alright?'

Kevin span around and punched Matt hard in the stomach. He dropped to his knees and threw up. Kevin leant down beside him and whispered menacingly into his ear. 'She's having the time of her life.'

Matt was hauled to his feet by Brian Chard and shoved forward by Kevin, towards the girl on the bench. Matt couldn't see her face; Andrew was still holding the top up.

Kevin pushed Matt forward from behind. The lads were chanting his name. Kevin leaned into him. 'We're a team. We won together, we celebrate together...' Kevin paused, and raised his voice and looked around the group. 'We are all in this together.'

The next morning Matt woke up in a state of confusion. Still dressed from the night before, his clothes crumpled and dirty on the floor, his head pounding so hard he had to hold it for fear of it falling off. He stood up a little unsteadily and tried to re-orientate himself. Then the realisation and memory hit him. He dashed into the bathroom and threw up. Splashing his face with water and cleaning his teeth with a hand that wouldn't stop shaking, he looked at himself in the small mirror that stood on the windowsill. The face that stared back at him belonged to a stranger. All hope and innocence had been torn away. Unable to bear the image any longer; he picked up the mirror and launched it against the door, shattering it into tiny splintered pieces.

Matt ran down the stairs, stepped into his shoes and out of the house. He didn't stop running until he reached

Bidbury police station. He paused just briefly before hurrying up the steps and into the building.

'Well, that's quite a story lad,' the detective opposite him said, 'are you sure you didn't imagine it?'

'No Sir,' Matt said seriously. He was in an interview room, sat across the table from the detective and a younger uniformed police officer. The detective had a comb over and a wispy moustache. He seemed very old to the young Matt, but was probably only in his late forties.

The detective looked at Matt's crumpled clothing. 'Easy to get it wrong after a heavy night out.'

'It happened.' Matt didn't sound or look any more convinced than the Detective was, could he have imagined it all? He had been very drunk.

'You wait outside; I'll call in the other lads to see if anyone supports the story. But we have had no reports of the crime come in...'

Matt sat in the station reception area and waited. One by one, his Rugby mates filed past him in and out of the interview room. As Andrew passed by, he clenched his fist in a threatening gesture, making sure that only Matt could see. Andrew was followed out by Kevin, who paused in front of him and turned his head to speak to the detective.

'He's a piss poor drinker; he'd already had a belly full. We tried to stop him, but...' Kevin shrugged his shoulders in a what can you do type way and glanced from the detective to Matt. 'Guess it was a bad trip.'

'You're a liar!' Matt said, jumping to his feet.

Kevin walked away with a satisfied smirk on his face.

The detective looked at Matt. 'I should caution you for wasting police time,' he said sternly, his moustache twitching. 'Now sod off. You're lucky I didn't call your parents.

Chapter 28

Lay off the drink and stay away from the ecstasy, it addles your brain...'

Matt stared at the man. He felt totally confused.

'Might already be too late in your case.' The detective added, chuckling to himself as he walked back into the interview room slamming the door.

In the days following the attack, Matt tried to justify his actions. He was drunk; he was young; he was threatened... he even tried to kid himself that the girls had been willing participants. But he knew it was all nonsense and there were no excuses, no justification and no forgiving his actions. So somehow he'd had to learn to live with the knowledge.

He expected to be arrested. Once the smug detective heard from the girls, then he would know the truth. But the police never came, and there were no reports in the papers of the rape. He tried to find the girls; he went back to the pub and hung around, night after night, for weeks. But he never saw them again.

His shame and self-loathing grew until one day he realised that the only way for him to stay alive and find some normality was to join the police force. At least then, he could lock away his shame and spend every day trying to rid the streets of scum like him. So that's what he did, and in the early days he had been vigilant and enthusiastic. Until cynicism and disappointment took over and he realised that the likes of Andrew, Kevin and Brian still walked the streets, cocky and cunning and free to bully and abuse again.

MATT LOOKED at the book and he wanted to read on, but he realised he had no time. He had to stop her, to save her from the consequences of her actions. He flicked on through the book, past her journal, which gave an account of each hit.

CHAPTER TWENTY EIGHT

There was a newspaper cutting which showed the victorious rugby team with an editorial that listed each of their names. Another newspaper cutting was a small piece about the tragic suicide of a local girl. Matt didn't need to be a genius to guess that must have been Liz's sister.

At the back of the book there were files. A separate one for each hit, names, photos, addresses, life style the attention to detail was incredible. It must have taken years to plan. He stared at a picture of himself, at his life under the microscope, even a photo of Avril standing outside their house. All their habits, the times he usually went to the gym, the restaurants they ate in, the hours they worked, the details of his wife's affair with Brian Chard. So Liz knew more about his marriage than he did himself!

Right at the back of the book were pockets with keys. Several were missing. He pulled out the list of names from his pocket and started looking down.

Suddenly Sam and Craig burst through the door, he'd been so engrossed he hadn't heard them get home.

'What are you doing?' Sam demanded. 'I thought we had burglars.' She took in his grave expression. 'What is it? Is it mum? Is she alright?' Sam looked at the book and the cuttings and steps closer. 'What is all this?'

Matt looked at her sadly. 'I can't explain now.'

'Is it mum? Is she alright?' she repeated.

'Probably not. I need to find her... fast.'

He stood up and quickly checked down the list against the keys. He ignored the houses that he had crossed off, hoping that the occupants had taken his advice and changed their locks. His key was still in the pocket, so was James'. It left him with four possible targets.

His mobile phone rang, and he quickly answered it. 'What is it, Jen?'

Chapter 28

He listened while Jen told him about the latest victim. He didn't care about the details. 'Who is it?' he asked, cutting her off.

He crossed another name off his list. Just three options left.

'Where's mum?' Sam demanded.

Matt stared at the three remaining names. He had to make a decision and hope it was the right one. 'I think I might know,' he said, as he picked up the book and all its accompanying bits. He hurried to the door. 'No time to explain now.'

'I'm coming.' Sam said, rushing after him.

He ran out of the house and into his car. 'No, stay here,' he said. 'I'll deal with it.'

'Like hell,' Sam replied putting on her crash helmet.

'What's going on?' a bewildered Craig asked.

'Follow that car,' Sam said.

LIZ PARKED her blue Mini and walked slowly down the street. This time instead of heading for the front door, she walked past and kept going until she reached the end of the row of terraces. She ducked down an ally at the end and followed it round to the back of the houses. She counted her way along the rear garden gates until she found the target house, then she slipped into the garden closing the gate behind her and hurried to the back door.

MATT SAW Liz's car and slammed to a stop beside it. He was barely out the door before Sam and Craig pulled up alongside him. He adopted his sternest police inspector pose and voice and addressed the pair of them. 'You must wait here.' He looked at Craig, 'keep her safe.'

Craig nodded his head in understanding. Matt ignored the protests and questions coming from a confused and panicking Sam. He ran to the end of the terraces and into the alley. As soon as he was in the garden, he saw that the back door glass was smashed and it was slightly open. He pushed it forward and entered cautiously through the kitchen. He stopped to listen but heard no sound, so he crept forward carefully into the hall and from there into the lounge. As he stepped into the room, he was relieved to see clear carpet without a dead body. But the relief was short-lived as a gun was shoved into the side of his head.

'How did you know?' Liz said from behind him.

'Are you going to shoot me?'

'When did you know?'

'Not until today,' he said, turning slowly around to face her. He looked into her eyes; the gun was still pointed directly at him. 'Liz, let me help you.'

'You can't,' she replied. 'I have to do this.'

'You don't, it can end now. I'll cover it up, make it go away.'

He could see the pain in her eyes and it tore at his insides. Surely she wanted it to end?

'I have to do this,' she said, shaking her head sadly. 'Steve tried so hard to do it legitimately. He built files on everyone, he followed them, gathered evidence and every time one of them stepped over the line he 'helped' the police. He would send in anonymous evidence, find witnesses…' she fought back the tears. 'But the bastards kept getting off. What is it they say? The devil looks after his own?'

Matt took a small step closer, but despite her despair the gun stayed pointed at his head.

Chapter 28

'How can I live and love while the bastards who killed my sister and my husband walk free? Do you know Steve spent two years building a dossier against Trevor Neam?'

Matt knew that Trevor Neam had been Trevor Hillard back then, The team called him Hithard because once he'd smashed into another player on the field the poor guy would go down so hard he had to be carried off the field. Matt hadn't known him well but knew that his parents divorced and Trevor changed to Neam to take his mother's maiden name. Then he left Bidbury and moved to London.

'Neam built his financial empire on lies and fraud, and my husband put together all the evidence. He was charged, but the bastard had the money to buy and bribe his way out of the allegations. He walked free, and it broke Steve's heart. So he killed him...'

'But Neam died in a car crash.'

Liz looked at him sadly. 'So did my husband.'

'The same crash?'

She nodded her head. 'He gave his life. I promised him I would complete the work...'

'Liz, let me go after them. I'll get every one of them convicted and behind bars for something.' He paused thinking it through and made a decision. 'When I've got them all banged up, I'll put my hands up for the killings you've already done and get myself locked away.' He meant it, every word, and he was well aware what happened to police officers who served time in prison, but he didn't care and he needed to do something, anything to save her.

'Why would you do that?' she asked, clearly stunned.

'Because I love you, because I owe you, because I deserve it and because Sam needs her mother.'

They both fell silent while the implications registered. Liz lowered the gun and Matt reached out to take it. A noise from behind made him swing round quickly. He saw a flash of metal before a large frying pan crashed down hard on his skull and his knees buckled beneath him.

He could hear his name being called from somewhere far away. He liked the sensation of floating somewhere between being drunk and dreaming. But consciousness was winning him round. He opened his eyes and groaned at the throbbing pain in his head.

'Shit, Matt! What are you doing? Thought I had a burglar.'

Matt tried to sit up and Ivor, the man who had just hit him, helped him to his feet. His memory returned as the grogginess faded and he looked around him for Liz. Clearly she'd gone.

'Matt? What's going on?'

Matt looked at the man who was still holding the offending frying pan and wearing a cycling helmet. 'I think you just got lucky...'

'Lucky? Have you seen my back door?

Matt was already on his way out through the damaged door. 'You're alive aren't you...' he tossed over his shoulder as he hurried away.

He ran to his car, Sam was waiting beside it, pacing impatiently.

'What happened? I saw mum run out, I called to her but I don't think she heard me. I wanted to follow her, but...' she threw an angry glare at Craig. 'He wouldn't let me, insisted that we had to wait for you.'

'Which way did she go?'

Sam pointed straight ahead.

Matt mentally flicked through the pages of the book and the remaining names. He knew exactly where she was going.

CHAPTER TWENTY NINE

Andrew was sprawled out on the sofa, watching a Rugby match, a bottle of Stella in one hand and several empties at his feet. Bruce was outside in the garden, sat at the glass doors looking in. The door into the lounge opened just as England lost to France. Assuming it was his daughter, he hurled the bottle behind him. 'Piss off,' he shouted angrily without bothering to turn his head.

'Soon, after we've had a little party.' Liz said.

Andrew leapt to his feet. She hadn't bothered with the balaclava. The gun was pointed straight at his forehead. Steady and firm.

His eyes narrowed as he assessed her, 'I've seen you in town. Yeah, you're a copper.' He started to edge towards the door.

'Stay still.'

'Why. You're going to kill me, anyway,' he said, his bravado boosted by the alcohol.

'True,' she replied with a tense smile, 'but it hurts more if I put several holes in you first and make you bleed to death.'

CHAPTER TWENTY NINE

He stopped moving. His eyes darted around, seeking options.

She shot him in the shoulder.

He screamed out in pain. 'I didn't move.'

Liz shrugged. 'I decided to hurt you.'

Andrew was worried. The dog was at the window, barking and growling, but a thick pane of glass meant it couldn't help him. His bravado was slipping away, reality was hitting home. He was in the shit. 'I know who you are,' he said, staring at her intently as his memories began to form.

'I mean, I know why. I remember.'

'Good.'

He decided to try a bit of charm. 'You were such a pretty wench. It was just a bit of fun.'

'Fun!'

'Yeah, just got a bit out of hand, that's all.' He forced himself to smile, even though the pain in his shoulder was sending him insane. What he really wanted to do was launch himself at the bitch and turn her gun on her. God that would be something, teach her she couldn't mess with him. He'd be a hero. The man who rid the world of a serial killer...

'Fun?' Liz screamed at him, her own calm slipping away. 'You killed my sister.'

Andrew was surprised, then disbelieving. 'No way.'

'She never recovered. She killed herself; she jumped from a bridge a few months after.'

'Depression. It happens. You can't blame me for that. We were just a few lads partying.'

Liz sent a second bullet into the same shoulder. The impact and the pain sent him to his knees. Liz moved closer.

Chapter 29

She pulled a lipstick from her pocket and chucked it at him. 'Write sorry on the floor.'

He looked at her with barely concealed hatred. 'You're insane...'

She lifted the gun and looked like she was about to fire again.

He grabbed the lipstick, grimacing against the pain. 'Alright, alright...'

A noise from behind her sent Liz spinning round. Kylie was hovering in the doorway. A shocked Liz stared at her. Kylie quickly retreated.

Andrew took his chance. He lunged for Liz. He was fit and fast and caught her in a rugby tackle. She was thrown backwards. The gun flew from her hand. She was flat on her back with Andrew on top of her. The blood from his gun wounds was oozing through his shirt and dripping onto Liz. 'Well, here we are again, sweetie,' he hissed, his breathing laboured from the exertion of his attack. He knew his loss of blood was weakening him. He needed her gun, but it was out of reach.

They both looked up, surprised as Matt crashed through the door. Close behind him were Sam and Craig. Matt hauled Andrew off Liz.

'Shall I call the police?' Craig asked.

Sam dropped down beside her mother, looking horrified and terrified by the blood smeared across Liz's shirt.

'No,' Matt replied to Craig.

'She's hurt,' Sam cried.

Liz shook her head and hugged her daughter. 'No, it's not my blood.'

Matt dropped to his knees beside her. Their eyes met in silent understanding.

Andrew edged backwards. The attention was focused on

Liz. Sam and Matt helped Liz to her feet. Andrew knew that this was his only chance. He had the uncomfortable feeling that Matt wasn't there to save him.

Liz was on her feet. Matt touched the bloody patch. 'Are you ok? Did he hurt you?

Andrew's fears were confirmed. 'Me, hurt her? Are you insane? She fucking shot me!'

His dog was head butting the glass, but it was too far away for Andrew to reach the door to let him in.

Matt turned around to face him. Sam held onto her mother. Andrew managed to get himself across to where the gun fell. He reached down and grabbed it. He lifted it up and took aim, a sick smile spread across his face.

Liz saw what was happening, so did Matt.

Matt was closer to Andrew than he was to Liz, so he launched himself at Andrew, and lunged for the gun.

Liz manhandled her daughter out of the way.

Andrew fired a shot, the sound of another gun fired followed immediately. Andrew was thrown backward by the impact as a bullet hit him in the chest. He was stunned. What the hell happened? He stared across in disbelief. Everyone turned to look at the doorway. Kylie was standing in her dressing gown and slippers, holding the gun that he had hidden under his bed. The world was spinning, and he felt himself falling. He couldn't believe that it was all over, that he was dying, shot by his own fucking daughter.

MATT WAS AS SHOCKED as Andrew had been. He went to the girl and gently took the gun from her hand. 'Kylie, right?' He said, glad for once that living so long in the same place gave him access to information and gossip. He remembered picking her up once for shoplifting. When he knew who she

Chapter 29

was and saw how scared she was of her father finding out, Matt persuaded the shopkeeper not to prosecute and he let her off with a warning. The girl nodded her head; she was shivering violently as the shock set in.

Craig ran to Andrew and dropped down to his knees. 'I think he's dead.'

Matt nodded, he wasn't sorry, but he knew he had one hell of a mess to clear up now. His mind was racing through and rejecting options and possibilities.

Sam suddenly shouted as Liz slid down the wall, a trail of blood streaking the emulsion.

'He shot her,' Craig cried.

Oh dear god no, Matt cried in his head. He ran to Liz and gently laid her down onto the floor; he cradled her head in his arms. 'Get an ambulance,' he shouted at Craig. Craig was stationary and stunned. 'Ambulance. Now!' Matt demanded, shaking the young man into action.

Sam was sobbing as she held her Mother's hand.

Matt leant down to Liz, and whispered, softly and urgently. 'Don't leave me. Please don't leave me…'

'I have to,' she whispered back, struggling to speak.

It was bad; the police officer in him had seen similar bullet wounds before and knew that she was dying. But as the man who had only just found the love of his life, he was blind to the reality and he held her tight, willing her to defy death. 'No. It's over now. I can cover this. Keep you out of it. I can save you. I'll find a way.'

Liz managed to lift her hand and she placed a finger across his lips. 'Then do it for Sam,' she managed to say. She looked sadly at him, then turned her head to her daughter. 'I love you,' she said before slipping away.

Sam sobbed loudly. Matt wiped away his own tears, knowing that the grieving would have to wait. The sounds of

CHAPTER TWENTY NINE

sirens could be heard approaching. He had to think and act fast.

Matt put Liz gently down on the floor and looked around the room. Kylie was sitting on the floor staring at her dead father. Matt stood up and hurried to her side. He touched her shoulder gently. She flinched. Surprised, he let his hand drop. 'Your dad is dead.' He said softly.

'I know.'

'I'm sorry...'

Kylie dragged her eyes away from the corpse and looked up at him. 'I'm not.'

It was exactly what Matt wanted to hear. He looked across at Craig who was trying to comfort an inconsolable Sam. 'Craig...' he got no response. He shouted, loud and with as much authority as he could find. 'Craig...!'

Craig and Sam looked at him. He saw everything in the young girl's eyes that threatened to overwhelm him. But he knew he had to keep control.

'Craig, go to my car and get me the book, the big scrapbook. Hurry...'

Matt looked around him, assessing the situation as a plan began to form. Craig returned with the book. Matt took it from him and looked at the pair of them.

'We need to be quick.' He said, 'Craig, you've gotta get Sam out of here. Now! Take her home and when someone comes to tell you what's happened, you must act surprised.'

'No,' Sam cried, holding onto her mother's hand. 'I can't leave her.'

Matt looked at her and spoke more gently. 'Sam, we have to do this, it's for your mum. You have to trust me and do exactly what I say.'

Matt stood up, pulled a glove from his pocket and

started cleaning Kylie's gun. Then he put Liz's fingers around it and squeezed.

'Now go!' he shouted at them.

He helped Kylie to her feet as Sam and Craig headed for the door. 'I'm going to tell you exactly what to say. Ok?'

Kylie nodded her head; Matt started pulling pages from the book. Anything that was personal to Liz.

Kylie looked at her dead father and then at Matt. 'Will I go to prison?'

'Not if I can help it.'

CHAPTER THIRTY

Matt walked into his office. A newspaper was on his desk. The heading read – SERIAL KILLER DEAD - He looked down and allowed himself a satisfied smile. A large photo of Andrew dominated the page.

Jen approached. 'So it was a paedophile ring all along. You did well to work it all out and get to the right house in time. How did you know it was him?'

'Oh, Andrew always was the rotten apple in the barrel.' As he said it. Liz's face entered his mind, he smiled.

'What?'

'Clichés,' he said. 'Sometimes it's all about the clichés.'

'Still so many unanswered questions, though. I'm not sure it all adds up. I mean, how did that PC know what was going on? I know Andrew Martin's daughter said that she had confided in her, but the woman was only in town for a few weeks and what about the hair we found at Kevin's? Pretty sure forensics will match it with her DNA.'

Matt kept calm. He had always known that Jen would be the stumbling block. They all just had to stick to the story he had constructed and it would be alright. Whatever doubts Jen had couldn't be proved. Whereas his case, even though it had holes in it couldn't be disputed, since Kevin and Andrew were both dead and everyone else said what he had instructed them to say. 'I don't suppose we'll ever know the full story. Clearly it was all to do with the child porno ring that they ran. From what his daughter said Andrew had a big fight with Kevin, she hid on the stairs and heard them arguing and it was to do with Liz, apparently she had been to see Kevin earlier that day to question him…'

'But why didn't she report it? Get CID involved?' Jen said, interrupting.

'I guess she wanted proof. Kylie was very scared about what Andrew might do if he knew she had spoken to the police.'

'But we could have got social services involved…'

'Exactly. That's what she was afraid of. She didn't want to go into care. She was just a scared young kid and PC Bryant was doing her best to help.'

'Well, she screwed it up,' Jen said crossly.

Matt kept calm and carried on. 'In the argument Kylie heard Kevin say he wanted to pack up and go abroad for a while but Andrew said they had to front it out. Kevin left and shortly afterwards so did Andrew. I reckon Andrew got spooked by PC Bryant snooping around threatening to expose them, so he covered his tracks by taking them all out one by one. Shut down the operation so nobody was left alive to talk.'

Jen sat down on his desk; she looked at the paper and shook her head. 'It doesn't add up though. What type of PC blunders around on their own like this? And where did she get the gun from?'

Jen was like a sniffer dog that had picked up the scent. 'I

CHAPTER THIRTY

still don't believe his daughter didn't see or hear anything during the shooting. You'd think a couple of gunshots might have roused her.'

'Weren't you ever a teenager, Jen? Earphones and McFly? Let it go. Case closed. We've broken up a porno ring. Young Kylie is no longer afraid of daily abuse from her father, and we've stopped a serial killer. You saw all the files with the info he had collected about the victims, he even had all the door keys.'

'But...'

Matt held his hand up, he'd had enough. 'No more buts, Jen. The case is closed.'

He looked at her closely. She wasn't happy and he couldn't take the risk that she would shake it all up and not let it die. He had done his best to construct the story and make it fit the evidence, but he knew it wouldn't stand up to very close scrutiny. He hadn't wanted to pull out his trump card, but she left him no choice. 'Strange how quickly the press got hold of the story,' he said walking to his computer and keying in some details. 'My guess is we've got a leak.'

'Really? But who would do that.'

Matt glanced down at his screen. 'Saw you in town the other day. Got a new boyfriend?' He felt like a git, but he would do anything to protect Liz and Sam.

Jen looked uncertain; she didn't know which way it was going. 'Just a friend.'

'Yep, you looked pretty friendly.'

'Gov?'

Matt tapped his screen. 'Trouble with being new in town, you don't always know who the players are.'

He walked away, knowing that she would be around the desk and staring at the screen. A big picture and biography of the young hotshot reporter Dan would stare back at her.

Chapter 30

He paused at the door and turned. He was right she was looking at the screen in horror. 'Or when you're being played,' he added.

He was pretty sure she would let it drop now; if he needed it, he had the photo of her kissing the reporter. She was far too ambitious to risk being associated with a leaked story. Especially one that was big enough to hit the nationals. The Chief Inspector, although obviously concerned that a policewoman had died in the line of duty, had turned PC Liz Bryant into a hero, and he wouldn't be impressed to learn that a young DS was not only threatening to tarnish his feel-good story, but she was also possibly in bed with the press.

MATT DROVE to Milltown and parked his car. He walked to the dance studio entrance and went in, looking around him uncertainly. A woman was waiting for him. 'Dawn?' he asked as she approached him. He had seen her at the funeral but not been introduced. He hadn't hung around, afraid that he would lose control.

She nodded her head. She was like a porcelain doll. Pale, impossibly dainty and fragile looking. Despite perfect makeup, she had shadows under her eyes. He knew pain when he saw it, the same haunted longing that lingered at the back of his eyes and stared at him every day when he looked in the mirror.

'I got your message. You wanted to see me?'

Dawn handed him an envelope. Matt was confused.

'Liz gave it to me. She came to see me, that morning...' she paused, unable to say the words.

Matt took the envelope. She didn't need to say anymore. Matt knew that Liz hadn't expected to walk away from her actions. She knew she'd go to prison. She might even have thought she might die. He was close to tears himself to think that she had taken the time to leave him a message. Dawn suddenly leaned forward and hugged him tight. Surprised, he hugged her back.

When she stepped back, she looked at him 'she was my best friend,' she said and walked slowly back into the studio.

DAWN WATCHED Matt from the window as he walked to his car clutching the envelope. Tears streaking her makeup as they ran down her cheeks.

Phillip hung back in the doorway. He wanted to help, he just didn't know how. He walked across to the music, turned it on and then approached her.

As the music started, she turned to look at him. He smiled and took her hand. He pulled her into the middle of the studio and into his arms as they started to dance a waltz.

MATT WAS SAT in his car, staring at the envelope. His hand shook slightly as he finally tore it open and pulled out a single sheet of paper. He started to read...

If Dawn has given you this, I must be dead. I did it for my sister. I'm sure you've found the book and you now know the full story. For twenty years I was torn in two. Part of me building a life and a future for me and my lovely daughter Sam, and the other part of me planning and plotting how I could get revenge on the rapists with Steve. I had to wait until Sam was old enough to live and to cope with life without me.

Matt was angry, he was upset, and he was hurting. 'Oh, Liz...' he said aloud before he forced himself to read on.

You know that you were part of the revenge. What I don't

know is how I fell in love with you. You made me examine what I was doing. You made me wonder for the first time if there could be any redemption, to question if it is possible to forgive. The fact that you are alive to read this is answer in itself.

Matt couldn't go on. He stopped reading, threw the page onto the seat beside him and started the engine. He drove way too fast. He didn't care. He wanted to rewrite history. Go back twenty years and undo the events that had started the whole tragic disgusting drama. Or even just skip back to that final day. If only he had found a way to stop her from making the final hits. Or even if he'd intercepted her before she got to Andrew.

But time moved relentlessly forward, just as it always did, and Liz was dead.

Matt was surprised when he realised he was in the cemetery car park. But then where else would he go? He opened the door and was about to climb out of the car, but paused and reached across for the letter. He needed to finish it.

Watch out for my Sam. She was conceived that night in the bus shelter. Amongst all that pain and hatred, my beautiful little miracle....

Matt walked towards the graves of Melissa and Steve. Between the two graves was a small urn that contained Liz's ashes.

Sam and Craig were sitting on the grass, fresh flowers laid out in front of them, covering the space across and between the graves in a floral blanket of colourful sweet peas. Sam turned her head as he approached and gave him a small, sad smile. 'Mum's favourite,' she said, pointing to the flowers as Craig helped her to her feet.

Matt looked at Sam. The last words from Liz's letter were spinning in his head.

CHAPTER THIRTY

She could be yours. You know how much you like clichés, and wouldn't that be the ultimate one?

Sam walked across towards him. 'She liked you.'

Matt nodded his head. 'I know.'

Craig took Sam's hand, and they started walking away. Sam suddenly stopped and ran back to Matt. She leant forward and kissed his cheek; he hugged her tight for a second, then let her go. He watched as she took Craig's hand and they walked away.

Matt took the few steps towards the graves and looked down at the urn. He touched his cheek and smiled. 'I do like clichés,' he said.

The End

I hope you enjoyed reading **The Book of Revenge**. Here is an advanced peek at the first chapter from my next crime drama featuring DI Matt Mardell:

The Book of Murder

The Book of Murder

A DI Matt Mardell Crime Story
Matt Mardell has a dead girl in a jacuzzi and an ex-girlfriend who might be the killer's next target. Following a trail of deceit and corruption Matt finds himself hindered by his boss, by the press and by a past relationship with a woman who is now, twenty years later, an infamous Madam. He can't decide if she is a potential suspect or a potential victim. Either way, there is a chemistry between them that is both thrilling and terrifying. But the last thing Matt needs now is to rekindle a

love affair with a woman living on the wrong side of the law.

Chapter One

She giggled as she tripped up the stairs. Her head was spinning, and she felt fantastic. She wasn't used to champagne, at least not the good stuff. She'd drunk plenty of the cheap pretend bubbles and she could usually take her drink. Maybe it was the company. He wasn't like any man she'd ever been out with before, and she was dizzy with anticipation.

She glanced back over her shoulder and smiled seductively. He pulled her backwards into his arms. With another girly giggle, she wriggled free and ran up the remaining stairs to a door. Rummaging in her bag and pulling out a key, she looked up at the security camera and blew a kiss towards it, unlocked the door and pushed it wide open.

'Won't you get in trouble?' the man said, glancing up at the camera.

'It doesn't record or store, it's just so we can see who's in there.' She replied without pausing. She led him down a corridor, pushed open another door and flicked on a light as she hurried into a messy disorganised room. Grabbing two glasses and bending down to search in a cupboard, she reached to the back and came out with a half empty bottle of whisky. She straightened up and smiled triumphantly.

She poured a generous measure into each glass and handed one to him. He took the glass, swallowed the contents in one fast gulp, and dropped the glass to the floor. He reached out and pulled her towards him, his fingers fiddling with the buttons on her blouse.

She drank the whisky in a single swallow and removed

CHAPTER THIRTY

her top. She took his hand. 'Not here,' she said, moving across the hall and into another room. Without stopping to switch the light on, she led him through the darkness and through yet another door. They were in a large ensuite with a Jacuzzi in the corner. She turned on the taps and the motor and stripped off her remaining clothes.

Naked, she looked up at him and took a step closer. 'Your turn,' she said, her fingers tugging at his belt buckle.

He let her undo the belt. She felt her excitement rise. She held his zip and was slowly lowering it. His hand was in his jacket pocket.

Suddenly, in one fast movement, he had her held in a tight, unyielding grip. She couldn't escape, she could barely move. Her breath was being squeezed from her lungs. His face was very close, his eyes dark and staring intently into hers. She whimpered, a small shocked sound as the first sliver of fear sent a warning bolt into her brain.

She felt a sting in her arm. Short, intense and fleeting, like an insect bite. Followed by a warmth beginning its passage through her veins, her muscles and bones turning to liquid as she slid out of his arms and onto the floor.

Her eyes were heavy, her head was fuzzy.

He lifted her up and dumped her into the now full Jacuzzi. He leant across and turned the taps off. He looked at her again with an expression of regret before he left.

She heard his footsteps on the floor and heard the door close. The water was high and overflowing. She was sinking. She knew she had to keep her head above the water, but her body was unresponsive. She could see the taps were still running a little. A flash of panic helped her fight to the surface, but it was a brief and futile attempt at survival.

Her eyes closed as she slid beneath the rippling surface, and the warm bubbles swallowed her up.

Chapter 30

Linda also writes an eBook Soap Opera Series.

JASMINE CLOSE
Episodes 1 - 5 FREE HERE
The Soap Opera that you read

JASMINE CLOSE
Follow the lives - Experience the drama!

THERE ARE TWENTY-FIVE EPISODES. Each episode takes around 25 minutes to read.

Follow the lives and dramas of the residents of a brand new housing estate.

Perfect for your lunch break, short commute, or just to curl up with on the sofa or read in bed.

Victoria works in the show-home and she likes to know what's going on. She's nosy, bossy, and caring, with a husband who keeps going AWOL and a teenage daughter she's struggling to connect with.

Jenny is suffering from post-traumatic stress and the move to the new house in the new city will, according to her husband, Miles, make everything better.

Barry is the building site Foreman who is working to a schedule that keeps being interrupted by the half-naked ladies in apartment two who keep diverting his men away from their work.

Steve severed his spine in a car accident and, fresh from the Spinal Injuries rehab unit, he's trying to find his place in a world that is now much scarier in a wheelchair than it was when he could walk.

Sonia has a perfect family and a secret life while Belle

just wants to keep her children safe and Natasha and Ed are adjusting to life with a new baby who cries all the time.

The American, Brett Anderson, is on a brief visit to see his sister, but he might have found a reason to make him stick around for a while longer.

ABOUT THE AUTHOR

Linda Dunscombe is an experienced author who loves creating characters and weaving stories. You can find all her books on Amazon and you can connect with her on Facebook or via her website.

ALSO BY LINDA DUNSCOMBE

Book 1

Book 2

Book 3

Printed in Great Britain
by Amazon